To John —

MILLION DOLLAR VIEW

Written by
Silver Krieger

Drawings by
Keith DuQuette

"Think less. Feel better."
Um... working on it!

Silver

Printed in the United States of America at McNally Jackson Books, 52 Prince Street, New
York, NY 10012.

www.mcnallyjackson.com//bookmachine/million-dollar-view-silver-krieger

First Edition

ISBN 978-1-938022-21-0

For the good people of Park Slope, and for the rest of us

CHAPTER ONE

When Flynn Sharpe, newly hired real estate agent at the Brooklyn-based real estate empire Harmony Realtors, was summoned by Harry Harmony himself to be the point person in the "clearing out" of Aunt Muffin's, the last lesbian stronghold in Park Slope, he saw in his mind the image of a dog, squatting on its haunches, while its owner prepared his hand with a blue plastic *New York Times* home delivery bag.

He had never envied the Park Slopers he saw on a daily basis, dutifully picking up after their pooches. It was now as if he, in some way, had been handed a makeshift scoop of his own.

"It's a delicate situation," said Harry.

His son, Buzz Harmony, leaned back against Harry's desk, crossed his expensive Italian loafers and bared his teeth. He was looking forward to lunch at the Blue Ribbon where Jorge, the day bartender, would greet him by filling a glass with Grey Goose, skewering a green olive through its pimento center and positioning it in his glass at the perfect angle.

"What that means," continued Harry, leaning forward until his wide belly hit the desktop and a roll of fat deposited itself onto a pile of papers, "is that you – " here he paused, uncertain of exactly who he was speaking to (there was always some new guy, wet behind the ears, standing on his hind legs waiting for the bone of a new assignment to drop) "find a way to get The Lesbians out of there so the goddamn papers don't come down on us like a pack of dogs on a roast pig at a Superbowl tail-gating party."

Harry, a former movie producer who had returned to the family business after years in Hollywood, had already become well-known in the local media for his colorful metaphors, generally directed at those who opposed his massive development projects.

Flynn nodded. "I can handle it."

"The whole fucking block is ready to go except for The Lesbians. You know what I had to pay that old Italian to get out of his shoe shop? Then the Poles heard about the payment and said they wouldn't leave their customers without Kielbasa. Unless they got double that.

"So?" He looked at Flynn.

"So," said Flynn, "I find out what they want."

"I know what they *don't* want," said Buzz.

"BUZZ!"

"Dad?"

"You show…" Harry looked at Flynn.

"Flynn," said Flynn.

"Flynn The Property."

"Okay, Dad."

"And don't make it a big production. I don't want drama." Harry shook his head ruefully. "I never thought I'd say this, but I don't want an audience."

The atmosphere at the Blue Ribbon was subdued. By the time Buzz and Flynn had settled themselves at the bar most of the lunch crowd had gone. The dark, lush décor shielded them from the Fifth Avenue sunlight and the trickle of top shelf vodka could be heard above the muted sound of silverware being placed on thick linen tablecloths in preparation for the evening hours, when hordes of well-heeled patrons would group themselves around their eighty-dollar entrees like pigs at the trough.

"Cheers," said Flynn. He raised the glass to his lips. He had no desire to spend his lunch hour with the boss's son, but after unsuccessfully advancing the idea that perhaps they take a quick look at The Property first, he had followed Buzz into the restaurant and was concerned about getting back to the office to report to Harry.

Buzz didn't answer. He was sucking on an olive, his eyes below his expensive Caesar haircut darting here and there.

Flynn followed his gaze to the busboys and waiters.

"Whatever happened to waitresses?" he said.

Buzz drained his glass. "You stay here," he said suddenly. "I'll be right back."

Flynn watched as Buzz strode towards the stained oak doors. Through the plate glass window he saw him charge southward down the avenue.

"Another?" said Jorge, brandishing the shaker.

What the hell, thought Flynn.

Forty-five minutes later, Buzz still hadn't returned. Against Flynn's protestations, Jorge had insisted on "topping off" his drink multiple times, and as he checked his cell for the fourteenth time, hoping for bulletins of Buzz's whereabouts, he welcomed the spreading numbness that followed the initial warmth from the alcohol.

He was still sore from his morning workout. There were several reasons for that, he reminded himself. It wasn't that he wasn't in shape. He had been forced to give up his New York Health and Racquet Club membership and move back to his native Brooklyn and now, to his chagrin, he found himself alongside neighborhood bodybuilders heaving ancient barbells at a gym on Ninth Street. Not only that, but he had discovered that even if he had been able to endure the extended inhalation of sweat-soaked wall-to-wall grey carpet odor, no up-to-date running machines were available. Understandably, he had felt out of place with his useless two-hundred dollar running shoes, especially since it appeared that the only place one could run was away from the screaming seven year-olds dashing from the pool to the toilets and vice versa. So he had to resort to simple sit-ups and push-ups that had left his muscles hurting in places he didn't even know he had.

You get what you pay for, he thought, but the truth was, he no longer had the one-hundred dollars plus per month it took to belong to the Club. After he'd been laid off from his job as a financial analyst at Credit Suisse it was not only that but his apartment downtown and in fact the entire borough of Manhattan that he'd had to let go. The real estate gig only paid commission, so he was using his savings to supplement his meager income while he waited for the market to turn around and the bigger fish to return to the waters.

The new aches in his body had only been amplified by the fact that he now was sleeping on a futon mattress. His grandfather, who had fought in World War II, had rightly called futons the Japanese revenge. But that was unfixable since the platform of the loft bed he slept on was already too close to the ceiling, and raising the mattress height by only a few inches would make it that much more claustrophobic. Plus, his roommate let him use it for free.

Certainly a comedown but undeniably a blessing. He had heard through a trader who had also been laid off that there was some sort of list which, if he could get on it, would make it easy to find a cheap apartment or a roommate. He quickly realized that his definition of "affordable" had somehow been radically altered by his reversal of fortune. Apparently this list belonged to someone named Craig. Would Craig let him use his list? What would he owe Craig? Would this mean he would then be expected to be Craig's friend?

With further research he had discovered that the man behind this list was apparently some sort of do-gooder with no investors behind him to ratchet the entire enterprise up to another level and capitalize on its popularity. As a former employee of the financial sector, the news of its existence had initially irked him, but like an atheist who finds God at the wrong end of a gun, his need for assistance soon overtook what he had thought were rock-solid values.

And so with the help of his new-found unseen friend Craig he found himself a room with a guy much younger than himself who worked as a production assistant on movies. Barnaby's hours were completely unpredictable.

The apartment was in a converted factory building in the South Slope. The loft-like dwellings had been dubbed the "yuppie projects" by locals because of the widespread use of towels and sheets to cover the windows overlooking the street, as well as the various and sundry small objects such as a can of bleach or a bag of cat treats that pressed up against the glass to welcome the morning sun.

Each evening he could look forward to returning to this version of home sweet home, putting on his iPod and climbing up into the loft bed that was placed strategically above the bathroom, turning and twisting throughout the night in a doomed attempt to find a soft spot somewhere in the Pearl Harbor that was his bed. Thus his aching back. He was absolutely certain it was due more to the bed than to the push-ups.

Flynn let his eyes wander to the liquor across the bar and the richly appointed bottles that gleamed seductively in the low light: brown and green and gold, deep blue and silver, set like crown jewels under the mahogany-framed mirror, and then his gaze travelled upwards to see his reflection: a thirty-two year-old man with brown hair and blue eyes, terminally clean-cut, who looked no different than he had three months ago in Manhattan. Still in possession of his expensive suit and watch, and of course, the essential latest communication device …no one would know that he was living with a roommate in his early twenties, sitting in a bar like a patient pooch waiting for the boss's son to take him on his afternoon walk.

"Empty…or full?"

He turned towards the sound of the voice and a dark redhead who had seated herself at the bar.

"Excuse me?"

"Your glass. Half empty –" she pointed to his martini, "or," she held up her drink, "half full?" As she said this she seemed to accent the latter adjective by leaning forward and almost imperceptibly drawing in her well-toned triceps to lift her cleavage up and out towards where Flynn was sitting.

"Um…full?" What else could he say? Considering what he was looking at any other answer could be misinterpreted and offense might be taken. The woman looked familiar, somehow. Was she someone from his last job that he'd forgotten – although there had been so few women in finance he would almost certainly have remembered her – or, worse, someone he'd recently been introduced to at one of the frequent love-fests that took place between Brooklyn politicians and Harmony staff.

"Good for you. I look familiar, don't I?" the woman was asking. "It's not just these, I know," she said, gesturing towards the vortex of her breasts, "I'm better than that."

"You're –" said Flynn, "Dale – you were on –"

"Dale Shaw," she said, with the delightful slightly self-deprecating smile that had been seen by millions around the nation. "'Open Heart Surgery.'"

"Oh, yeah…right, you starred with that actor, the one with the sex addiction –"

"Which one?" she said. "You'd be surprised how many of those men are sick."

Her long hair swung around her shoulders.

"That would work 'cause you played a doctor, right?"

"Ha-ha. We're filming my new show right up the block. A Brooklyn townhouse is apparently a setting of interest now. God knows why. Park Slope is the most boring place on earth. The place is crawling with dads and their strollers with baseball caps pulled down around their ears like horses with blinders. Not even a glance and I have a *fantastic* rack. Sometimes men can be too well-trained. And what about you?"

"I don't have much of a rack, I'm afraid."

"Ha-ha. No stroller?"

"No stroller."

"Oh thank God." Dale took a gulp of her drink and set it on the bar in front of her. "I thought you might be hiding one under a table. I've seen worse."

"No, unfortunately. Or, fortunately…" Flynn's voice trailed off as his cell began to play the Mission Impossible theme song.

"I have to take this," said Flynn.

Dale raised one eyebrow just slightly in the inquisitive manner that only increased her attractiveness and had been seen by millions. "No sweat by me," she said, and produced her own gadget which she checked and laid on the bar.

"Talk to me." Harry's voice boomed out through the tiny speaker.

"Well," began Flynn.

"Where the hell is Buzz? I called that son-of-a-bitch and he didn't answer. He's like a demented beagle; you can't keep that bastard in the yard."

"He's – in a meeting," said Flynn, improvising.

"In a meeting?" said Harry with a mixture of disbelief and repugnance. "What kind of a meeting?"

"With – The Lesbians," Flynn said awkwardly.

"Oh. So how's it going?"

"Well, I think," said Flynn.

"Be careful," said Harry. "They're very touchy. I should know. My daughter's one."

"Oh…good," said Flynn.

"Yeah. I always told her, since Day One, most men are scum. Stay away from them. Luckily she found herself at an early age."

Dale was mouthing something at Flynn and pointing to the back of the restaurant.

"Absolutely, sir," Flynn replied. His eyes followed her as she slid off the barstool and undulated towards the booths and bathrooms. "People should…be allowed to be real."

"Park Slope is the most boring place on earth."

"What? I'm in my car, I can't hear you."

"I just said…"

"Hold on, I'm getting another call."

Flynn heard the click of the line being put on hold. What was he going to say if Harry asked him anything else about the day? He wasn't getting paid (assuming he got a deal done) to shoot the shit with a hot redhead, regardless of the fact that it was Buzz's fault. Maybe, though, some of her movie pals were looking for a good deal on a townhouse. Fuck that! What about a mansion on the park? Flynn began to sweat. *Holy shit! Seven point five million…that sounded about right…standard broker's commission…*

"Moron!" Harry's voice came over the line.

Flynn froze.

"Idiot who's working for us in Red Hook calls me up, says 'Hey, it's me.' I said, 'Me'? Who's 'me'? When you're me I'll let you know.' Where were we?"

"Your daughter."

"Listen, Jim, call me later at my house in Long Island. I'm about to go into a tunnel."

Flynn put his phone down. Well, today was shot. He stood up and reached for his wallet and looked around for Jorge and then remembered Dale. Her pink phone was next to her wineglass and a large buttery-looking leather bag. She had probably gone to the bathroom. It would be rude to go now and leave her things unguarded, especially since he had realized she might be his gateway to meeting the kind of people who could buy whatever they wanted regardless of the asking price. Maybe this day hadn't been wasted after all.

At that moment Dale emerged from the back. Hips swaying, she expertly navigated her way among the scattered patrons still lingering at their tables.

"You have a great walk," said Flynn, as she joined him at the bar. "You looked like you were on your way to pick up an Academy Award."

"Pretty soon," said Dale.

"Empty, or full?" said Flynn.

"I'm sorry?"

"The room."

"It doesn't make a difference," said Dale. "You always have to be on. Oh, look," she pouted. "I left my pretty cell phone all by herself."

"It's okay. I was watching out for…her."

"Mmm. She's so pink, and yours is so black. Don't they look cute together?"

Barnaby was on the kitchen island chopping up carrots and green peppers and making coffee when Flynn got home. Barnaby was an intense young man who wore black t-shirts and wire-rimmed glasses and took his job as a production assistant very seriously.

He would stand like a sentry on the perimeter of the protected ground where the movie was being shot, walkie-talkie at the hip, eyes expertly scanning the terrain for potential interference. He had become adept at informing drivers and pedestrians alike that there were, for example, alternate routes to Methodist Hospital. When filming took place on a residential block and incredulous residents were told that the wait to access their home might be twenty minutes or more, Barnaby (albeit with a policeman or two lurking in the background) was polite but inflexible.

"Hey," said Flynn, as he came in the door.

"What's up."

Flynn watched as Barnaby, who was vegan, added both the coffee and the vegetables, along with some ice, together in a blender and flipped the switch. A sound like a high-powered drill filled the room.

"You going to drink that?" said Flynn, as he watched Barnaby pour the brown lumpy liquid into a glass.

Barnaby nodded. "Nutrients and stimulants. It's an all night shoot."

Flynn raised his eyebrows. He hoped they had Port-O-Potties on the set. "Well, good luck with the filming. I guess it makes it easier when there's nobody around."

"Fuck no," said Barnaby, who tonight was wearing a Rotting Sheep Corpse T-shirt, one of his favorite vegancore bands. "That's when the real freaks come out."

"Oh," said Flynn. "So you're filming in Manhattan?"

"Manhattan?" Barnaby scoffed. "Hell no. This isn't mainstream shit. I only do that for the money so I can make art. This is indie. We're in the Gowanus." He took a draw of the drink while Flynn tried to mask

Barnaby was an intense young man who wore black t-shirts and wire-rimmed glasses and took his job as a production assistant very seriously.

a grimace. "Nobody that matters shoots in Manhattan anymore. The place is one big fucking mall. You might as well film in Minnesota." He drained the last of his coffee veggie smoothie.

"I think my company did some developments in SoHo," said Flynn. "People have to shop," he offered.

"I was all about New York ever since I saw 'Taxi Driver' when I was ten," said Barnaby, with a dreamy look in his eye. "They ruined it now, though. Where the hell did you grow up, by the way?"

"Brooklyn," said Flynn. "What about you?"

"Minnesota."

Flynn emptied out his pockets on the table under his loft bed. Among the detritus of the day was a receipt from Starbuck's, a ticket from a shoe repair shop on Flatbush, and Dale's cell phone number, quaintly written on a napkin. Maybe he'd give her a call tomorrow, he thought, as he undressed and began the ascent to his place of slumber. She was definitely gorgeous, no doubt about that. But so was his ex-fiancé. And apparently also somewhat of a lush, just like she had been. He had been a gentleman and insisted on picking up the tab for both of them. When it came, after Dale had already left, it was for one hundred and six dollars. Six months ago it wouldn't have mattered.

Right before he slid off into sleep he remembered that Harry had told him to call him in Long Island. He was too tired to do anything about it now. He drifted off into a dream where the Brooklyn skyline was full of water towers filled with coffee. Then he smelled something awful and looked down and saw that he was waist deep in the waters of the Gowanus Canal.

He woke up to the sound of the toilet flushing beneath his bed. The smell was all too real. Apparently Port-O-Potties were not included in the budget of independent films.

Chapter Two

Flynn awoke the next morning with a huge hangover and a renewed sense of purpose. There was nothing like finding yourself a bit player on a twenty-three year-old's version of a reality TV show to recall old bits of advertising wisdom such as "Just Do It" and "Make It Happen." As he stood in the shower and let the hot water beat down around his neck and shoulders he determined that he was going to have to strategize more effectively if he wanted to get ahead.

He pulled on his jogging shorts and headed out the door. It must have rained sometime during the night. The smell of wet grass drifted up to him from the newly dampened earth and the cool breeze soothed his forehead. He jogged down Seventh and turned up towards the park on Ninth Street, ready to take the rising slope ahead of him.

"Morning," he shouted to a well-dressed man who was walking his two small pure-bred dogs, but the man declined to answer.

He found himself puffing just a little bit as he came upon the monument that guarded the entrance to the park. As he joined the other early morning joggers and expensively dressed racing bikers, he reflected that if he didn't "make it happen" soon, he'd no longer be part even of the Brooklyn elite, let alone Manhattan. Pretty soon his morning ritual would be gone; he would no longer run among the lawyers and brokers who now dominated the Prospect Park loop. Sure, if worst came to worst, his father would welcome him back to the house in Bay Ridge, where he would have the joy of watching his father's second wife verbally abuse him.

He sped by a running mom with a three-wheeled no doubt astronomically-priced stroller, her baby's head jiggling up and down on its delicate neck along to her rhythm, and overtook five or six men with corporate logos on the backs of their T-shirts. Really, the consequences of being without money were potentially worse than he had thought. Everyone knew that despite what lip service might be paid to the idea that, as his father had said to him when he was growing up, "you're not better than anybody and nobody's any better than you," people as a rule judged books by their cover. In fact, he told himself, his jaw tightening, if people were books most of their readers wouldn't get beyond the first paragraph.

Like it had been with Constance, his ex-fiancée. It had undoubtedly been because of his good looks and the fact that he pulled in six figures that she had shown her initial interest. Or rather, made him the target of her conquest. It was as if, based on what she had gleaned by flipping through a catalogue, she had bid on and then won him at auction. But Constance had behaved like an experienced collector and, after unwrapping him and putting him on display in a position of relative prominence, had moved on to fresh prospects. Not so much other men as other pursuits of interest such as becoming friends with people that other people thought were important. The fact was that she had been content with knowing nothing more about him than what could be seen on the surface.

He slowed his run as the road sloped downwards and the lake and the toddling ducks came into view. A haze had enveloped the sun, making the still water appear placid and gray.

Harmony Realtors was housed in a new glass building constructed by the company itself, and it towered over the surrounding skyline. It was the only development in years that had somehow magically been granted the right to loom high enough over Prospect Park to be seen from inside its pleasant meadow. It stood out like an unwelcome guest at an exclusive gathering to which only the ornate pre-war apartment buildings and nineteenth century mansions that dotted Prospect Park West had been invited. You could almost hear their disapproving whispers as the wind blew among the trees.

The Manhattan-like structure had been planned to house a combination of offices and residential units, but due to the uncertain economy, the full completion of the project had had to be put on hold. The exclusive use of glass only amplified its current desolation: as if a catastrophic act of nature had caused a wall to fall, haphazard tableaus of furniture and people were exposed for anyone who cared to look.

On the street level was the realty office, along with a deserted mini convention center decorated with drab couches, tables of faux wood, and empty executive chairs. One floor above that was the only occupied apartment; a couple from Manhattan had been lured by the prospect of living among celebrities who were predicted to seek the status of the name-brand architect, and had raced to be the first, and as it turned out, the only inhabitants.

With no one living above the second floor the elevator had been shut down, making access to the rooftop pool and gym available only to those who were willing to climb the thirty stories to use the Stair Master. No one fit the bill and so that too had been closed. The awning that stretched into the sidewalk read "Harmony House" in a white, flowing script.

Flynn arrived at the Harmony headquarters to find two of the brokers engaged in their favorite sport of betting on how many birds would hit the sheer glass walls of the Harmony each day and go to meet Big Bird in the sky.

"Twenty-three in one fucking day yesterday. Yes! Pay up, bitch," said Kev.

"Didn't it promise that in the prospectus?" said his friend Seth, laughing. "'Designed with maximum bird slaughter in mind'? That rocks. I wanna have a band and call it Maximum Bird Slaughter."

Flynn pushed past them to his desk and dropped his jacket on the chair.

"Flynnie! What's up?" said Kev.

"Apparently the number of heartless bastards in the universe," said Flynn.

"Well, look who didn't get laid last night," said Kev.

"Actually, I could have."

"You were out on Third Avenue after dark?"

"Right. Think 'Open Heart Surgery.' Now think the hottest woman on the show."

"Dale? Dale Fucking Shaw? You almost fucked her?" Seth was practically panting.

"No, I bought her a drink, dickhead. Drinks, plural. Many of them."

"You got her blasted and didn't visit the cathedral?" said Kev.

"What?"

"Oh, sorry, man. Just old Catholic school code."

"Brilliant. Well, no, I didn't."

"What the not fuck!?" said Kev. "Oh, well. Next time you're being a homo give her my number. Wow. Dale Shaw. Bonus!"

"Boner!" said Seth.

"Bonus Boner!" they said together, and high-fived each other.

And I thought traders were the biggest assholes on earth, thought Flynn.

Predictably, Buzz was not in his private office.

Fuck it. Flynn scrolled through the new listings and checked his emails. He'd check out Aunt Muffin's on his own. Buzz, the idiot, had never shared the address with him beyond the fact that it was on Fifth Avenue somewhere below Ninth Street, but how difficult could it be to find a bakery? A new rallying cry had succeeded the mantras of the 80's: Just Google It. And so it would be.

Harry's door was open and Flynn could hear him ranting about some deal gone wrong.

"The Hasidim? That piece of shit let the Hasidim manage the property? Does he know how much revenue we're going to lose on Saturdays?"

Flynn silently thanked the Jews for their piety as he slipped by unnoticed.

As he left the office, Flynn slung his jacket over his shoulder with one hand and with the other called Buzz's cell. As a financial analyst his interaction with people had been minimal. He'd sat in front of a computer all day. He was beginning to think that electronically monitoring multi-million dollar trades was a breeze compared with making the simplest arrangements with a human. But if Buzz was going to be a dick he'd just go himself. Ultimately his loyalty was to Harry, not his spoiled and flaky son.

"Yeah, it's Buzz. Leave it."

"Hey," he said, at the sound of the beep, "it's Flynn." Keep it short and diplomatic. "We must have missed each other yesterday. Let's make a time to see the Property today. I'm just leaving the office but let's try to make it before noon." There. He'd made an effort to involve Buzz, as if anyone gave a crap. That way when he made the report there was no way it would look like he'd cut him out. But you know what? After today he was done covering Buzz's lazy ass.

Feeling satisfied with his new-found freedom he decided that he would splurge at Starbucks and go for a Grande Café Americano rather than the Tall he had budgeted for.

He stood on line at the First Street location. When he'd first left Brooklyn for Manhattan, he'd missed the mom and pop stores he'd grown up around, the friendly banter and special attention, the way the owners had watched him grow up and remembered his mother. Lacking a choice in the financial district, he'd adapted to the relentless sameness of the chain stores. The servers might constantly change, and the size and layout might differ slightly, but the repetitive décor, lighting and music created the illusion of familiarity.

While he waited, Flynn used his cell to Google Aunt Muffin's. It seemed many aunts were happy to offer their muffins - Aunt Blanche's Blueberry, Aunt Evelyn's Cranberry and Chutney, Aunt Hilda's Health Spelt – but only online, not in a store, and when he Googled Brooklyn, all that came up was Aunt Butchie's in Bay Ridge.

As he went through the rote steps of placing his order he contemplated this newest obstacle, and when his turn finally came, it occurred to him that asking one of the servers was the obvious solution. Of course! Why hadn't he realized it before? People in stores always knew their competitors, and a bakery like Aunt Muffin's would undoubtedly offer coffee along with its muffins. Plus, Starbucks had muffins too. He'd had them, and they weren't bad at all.

An employee with a tag that read "Sarah" looked like a likely target, with her strawberry blonde hair and Midwestern good looks.

"Excuse me," said Flynn, speaking into the millisecond pause before the 'next guest' was called, "but I'm looking for a place around here called 'Aunt Muffin's'? I was wondering if you might know where it is."

"Oh, I don't know," she said. "I really don't know the area. I just commute here from Staten Island, you know? So... I really don't know much about what's around here...except...there's a Barnes and Noble's a couple blocks down."

The Park Slopers on line pawed the ground impatiently.

"Oh, wait," said another server, "isn't it that place across the street?"

"That's *Connecticut* Muffin," put in the boy barista, as he steamed milk.

"Doesn't Barnes and Nobles sell muffins too though?"

"I dunno. I know they sell Starbucks."

"Next guest!" called Sarah.

So much for knowledgeable neighbors. His best bet for finding the place, then, would be to make a loop by going up Seventh Avenue and then down to Fifth and back around towards Union Street. He sipped his Americano gratefully through the plastic top. Thanks to the hit of caffeine, his hangover threat level was dropping from orange to yellow.

As he made his way down Seventh Avenue, Flynn began to do what was unthinkable for a New York native: he began to stroll. The warm sun and cool breeze blowing between the park and the river plus the strong taste of the coffee gradually made everything appear kinder and brighter. There was something about the streets and the churches and the fact that there were still stores like the barbershop on Fourth and the fish place on Third that was calming and like a small town. By the time he got to Ninth Street, he was whistling.

The plethora of competing real estate agencies that now dotted the avenue barely concerned him. After all, Harmony Realtors' assets made them look amateurish; nevertheless, he stopped at the corner to scrutinize the listings at Windsor Worthington-Fitzwalden. The word on the street was that it was owned by a Yaakov Schlepstein. What he saw both encouraged him and filled him with disbelief. The prices were outrageous. He himself would never in a million years be taken for that. He really wondered at the judgment of those who had, but that, of course, was now a plus for him. It was all about being on the right side of the register.

He eye-balled a listing for 4.5 mil, automatically calculated commission, and nearly smacked himself in the head. What the fuck was wrong with him? Dale Shaw was loaded, so what if in more ways than one, and how could he have back-burnered her and her rolling-in-it friends? No doubt, the Slope was hot as a frying donut, and before he knew it, he had flipped open his cell, extracted the crumpled napkin she had given him, and entered her number.

Her voice-mail featured her trade-mark purring intonation, and he took a deep breath, hoping to convey both an appropriate level of professionalism that she would remember when he broached the subject of available deals, and at the same time a confident and sexy message leaving open the nature of their relationship:

"Dale, hi, it's me…here… the one with no stroller? Ha-ha. We met yesterday at the Blue Ribbon bar. Really great meeting you. I'd like – *love* to get together for another couple of drinks and show you the neighborhood. There's some great out-of-the-way places I'd really like to take you. And we can *absolutely* keep it between ourselves. It must be rough for you with everybody breathing down your neck all the time. But *I'd* like to. Ha-ha."

He clicked off and breathed a sigh of relief. Not bad. A pretty good replay of the type of banter they had engaged in as he'd lingered and the afternoon had worn on and the drinks had continued to flow. She'd call him. She'd been the one who'd started the conversation, after all. And if not, he'd just call her again. That's the way most of the women he'd dated had liked it, he as the pursuer and they as the quarry.

He was *finally* starting to kick ass. With his psyche in second gear, Flynn crossed the street with a slight bounce to his step. *Hmm…Brooklyn Industries…not really his style, but…a backpack from this place might be in order.* Flynn peered through the window into the recesses of the store. The look was more casual and definitely more edgy than what he was used to, but in Park Slope, he supposed, do as the Slopers do. A backpack and maybe even a jacket to go with it. It'd be an investment. Brooklyn was hip now and hip done in the right way and with the right people meant money, and so why look like he just got off the boat from Manhattan? In the Zone! At last he was thinking right…

The reminder alarm on his cell was going off crazily and jolting him out of the pleasant feeling and all of a sudden he realized that he'd completely forgotten he had an appointment – in about two minutes - to show a potential client a condo on the rapidly evolving far Western reaches of the Slope.

Fuck! Shit! Way to be successful! He began to run, the coffee in its container sloshing up and around and bubbling out of the hole on the top and he nearly knocked over a Latino grandmother who was out with her cart for her morning grocery shopping. He ditched the overpriced coffee into the gutter and as he made it to Fifth Avenue he had to slow down because there was no breeze down there, it was fucking hot with hardly any trees, so much so that even though he was late Flynn breathed a sigh of relief and came to a halt when some dilapidated scaffolding erected over boarded-up brownstones extended for nearly half a block, offering him a refuge from the white-hot sun. It was dirty and disgusting but an oasis in the concrete desert and his head, for Christ's sake, was going to explode and he had to stop. In the damp darkness he paused to catch his breath and suck in the slightly fetid but moist and cool air.

It was then that he noticed a familiar-looking Porsche convertible parked just steps away. At the same time he heard the unmistakable sounds of male orgasm coming from steps leading down to the basement of one of the brownstones. Moments later Buzz emerged, zipping up his fly and wearing the same Armani suit he'd had on the day before. He was followed by a short, muscular Italian. Flynn flattened himself against the wall so fast that he knocked his hangover-ridden skull against the scaffolding's supporting pole.

"Thanks, man," he heard Buzz say.

"Dicks like yours are the whole reason I do this," said the man, who was wearing tight jeans and a tighter, blindingly white tank on top of which dangled several gold chains.

"Everyone says that," said Buzz. He sat in his car and slammed the door shut and pulled out without so much as a glance behind him as his trick gazed after him like a dog abandoned by its master.

Seriously? thought Flynn. He crept out from his hiding place.

"Hey," said the man, catching sight of him. "What's up?" His eyes traveled down from Flynn's face to his crotch. "Wow," he said. "Dicks like –"

Flynn held up his hand. "Gotcha. Thanks anyway."

Hands on her hips, Mrs. Carl Haliburton V surveyed the worn and dirty hardwood floors, then let her eyes travel up the dingy white walls to the peeling plaster above.

"Surely," she said, "you don't expect me to think of these – things – as moldings? Moldings, my dear, were not bought at Home Depot in 1983." She moved over to a window and laid a gloved hand on the sill, then quickly removed it after seeing the amount of soot that clung to her fingers.

"And a courtyard," she said, looking down, "does not moonlight as a garbage dump. Oh, no…I'm afraid…no," she continued, before Flynn could reply. "Even my daughter, who I doubt ever opened a book in the four years of that over-priced mill they call a college, deserves a better graduation gift than this."

"The neighborhood is very desirable," said Flynn.

"Desirable? Darling, don't waste my time. If I wanted Ivy to live among auto shops and abandoned American Legion outposts, I would have left Carl to move in with that nicely muscled mechanic who used to fix my car when we were in Texas."

"It's – a pretty good price for Park Slope. Five hundred seventy-five for a junior one bedroom. It'll probably be gone by Monday," said Flynn, repeating a real estate Cliff note sales pitch, in a final attempt to woo her.

"For five hundred and seventy-five thousand dollars, I could buy an entire Senate sub-committee. You know, we Southerners aren't as stupid as you think."

"Oh, no – I mean –" Flynn floundered, "we, uh, show the same apartments to everyone."

"And they buy them? Then I suppose Northerners *are* as stupid as *we* think."

She headed for the door, then paused and looked at Flynn.

"You seem like such a nice young man. Handsome, too." She shook her head. "And here you are spending your days trying to get people to believe that an outhouse is a mansion. Stay in this profession long enough and you'll be ready for politics."

"I only just started," said Flynn, warming to her motherly tone.

"I don't think you're very good at your job. That's a compliment, sweetheart."

What a great day. Not. No sale, the nauseating sound and sight of Buzz, and not one message on his cell. Flynn, hands in his pockets and feet scuffing the sidewalk, trudged back up the same slope he had taken with such confidence that morning. Mrs. Haliburton had been right, after all. Right now, he didn't feel very successful.

Facts and numbers were easy. The research and advisement skills he'd used as he analyzed the ups and downs of the stock market had seemed like second nature. It was nothing like reading a person so you knew just what to say to get them to do what you wanted. And that seemed to be a prerequisite if you wanted to win in this game.

Looking down, he saw the leftover rain in the gutter, mixing with the dirt of the city. His mother, before she started drinking, had always shown him the rainbows that oil slicks formed on the water.

But maybe even that idea, of the way she had been when he was really small, was like those chalk drawings on the sidewalks in Mary Poppins. The kind of world you want to jump into but it washes away in the rain and you wonder if it was ever there at all.

A bright, peeling "brrrrinnnnggg" startled Flynn out of his reverie. A telephone was ringing. Not a cell phone, but an honest-to-god old-fashioned rotary phone. It had to be. There was no other sound quite like it. Flynn looked around him for source of the disturbance, but to no avail.

The ringing continued. Insistent, louder than any ringtone, annoying. Finally, he saw it, squatting like an insect he wanted to slap, on the second floor fire escape of an unusually narrow three-story building across the street. It was indeed primitive – he could see it from here – large and black, with its square body and clunky receiver, round dial and trailing cord.

It continued to ring until the window behind it finally opened and a young woman with shiny dark hair hanging half over her face poked her head out. Flynn saw her reach out and fumble with the receiver, knocking it off its stand before managing to pick it up.

The small streets of the Slope had a way of bouncing sounds off the walls.

"Mmm?"

Pause.

"Mmm."

Another pause.

"Mmm-mhu…Of course I'm asleep. What time is it? It's noon? Is it important? No, it's okay. Can you hang on a minute?"

Moments later a sequined turquoise slipper felt for a foothold on the iron slats, and then she emerged, wearing a blackish blue short raincoat flung over what looked like a cross between a sundress and a vintage nightgown in filmy yellow. Flynn thought he saw her wince in pain as she sat down and propped her feet on the fire escape steps.

"Hey, I'm back. Yeah, of course I remember Benjamin and Philip. I know. I remember. You were really upset both times…You what? You found out your rising sign was Sagittarius, not Capricorn? No, I know it's important, honey. Calm down. Of course. No, no, you're right. Maybe that was why it didn't work out with them." She kicked off one of her slippers and began massaging her ankle. She sighed loudly. "Oh, God. No, I didn't mean anything by that. I'm just really tired, Lorelei. From working. All night. Setting up the studio for the open house…No, I don't think you should call either one of them. No, I'm not mad. Just don't sit inside obsessing, okay? Come to the open house later. Bring some beers, it'll be fun. Around eight. Okay, hon. Talk to you later. Feel better."

She had barely replaced the receiver on its hook when it rang again.

"Hello? Who? Zack? I'm sorry, I don't – oh, the bar in Red Hook. You were the one with the thick black glasses? Right… No, I totally remember you. Tonight? No, I can't. What? I can't hear you. I said I can't – I think we have a bad connection…Excuse me? No, I meant the phone. We have a bad connection over the *phone*. Well, fuck you too."

She hung up and from across the street Flynn could see her shaking her head. "Christ," he heard her say out loud. "Sometimes I feel like I'm living in a nut house."

She got up and went back inside, leaving behind the forgotten slipper.

A slow smile spread across Flynn's face. He could certainly relate to *that* sentiment. Her friend Lorelei must be one piece of work. Maybe he should set her up with Kev or Seth. And that guy Zack sounded like a winner. He snorted with laughter, and then realized he couldn't remember the last time he'd found something funny.

A very small black and white cat popped up from behind the potted plants on the window sill and began making its way towards the unknown object that had invaded its territory. Its tail swished back and forth, and then it pounced on the slipper, sending it tumbling down to the sidewalk, after which it glared down at its lost prize and began to yowl loudly.

Flynn wondered if he should do something... it was none of his business... but it was such a *cute* slipper, and any minute now it would be crushed by the hurrying heel of the next pedestrian.

He crossed the street and, under the watchful feline gaze, picked it up and put it in his suit jacket pocket. The girl was really, actually, kind of adorable. This could be awkward...

He smiled and shrugged at the same time, then went to the doorway.

It was then, with his finger an inch away from the rust-encrusted doorbell, that he saw the barely visible lettering on the darkened storefront that was the ground floor of the building:

AUNT MUFFIN'S

And under that, a sign:

TONITE
LEATHER EXTRAVAGANZA!

Slipper forgotten, Flynn peered through the glass. It was a nighttime place, obviously, not a place to get muffins at all.

Strange name for a place that clearly was no bakery. Well, thought Flynn, if this was how the ladies partied more power to them! He was sure it was nothing like the typical man's drinking hole, rather very civilized, and a vision passed before him of librarian types with their black-rimmed glasses reading and talking inside, maybe indulging in a glass of wine.

He'd thought before that he'd have his conversation with The Lesbians over a cup of home brewed coffee and a muffin served by stocky women with ruddy faces, white aprons and short grayish white hair, as he had originally imagined them, but educated and sophisticated types such as these might prove to be were certainly okay too. Sure, like everybody else he'd seen and heard about various actresses or other famous women on TV talking about or actually being lesbian, but as he never paid much attention to such things, and since during his time in the financial sector the Wall Street Journal had been an actual business paper, he hadn't registered much about this new emergence of chit-chat regarding women sleeping with women. Men were "out" and gay now too quite commonly, that had been going on for even longer, you would have had to be dead not to notice the brouhaha that periodically touched down in different points in the United States like tiny tornados, sweeping politicians and screaming activists on both sides into the vortex of debate over whether or not someone should be allowed to police your bedroom, which you'd have to be crazy, Flynn always thought, to agree to.

Well, but "Leather Extravaganza"? What was that? Whatever. He'd figure it out. The important thing was, now that he'd located his target, he execute his task ASAP. Thanks to Buzz's incompetence, he still didn't know what the owners had already been offered, and, after his lie to his boss about Buzz's non-existent meeting, it was too late to ask Harry the exact nature of the previously proffered deal, he would only come off looking like he hadn't done his homework.

No biggie. It couldn't be too difficult, he reasoned, turning away. He assumed that a holdout usually wanted more money, and why not give it to them, after all? If he was in their position, he'd do the same. When your ship comes in, it should be a yacht, not a rowboat. He was relieved that he was finally getting on track with his mission.

He became conscious that he was sweating. The grey fabric of his suit was soaking up the sun like a black umbrella at the beach. He contemplated the rest of his day. He only had one showing later this afternoon. Maybe he'd go back to Brooklyn Industries and trade in his business attire for the hipper look he'd been thinking about earlier. It would make him blend in better when he returned to Aunt Muffin's to have his talk with the owner.

The clothes that he was wearing now would have fit in perfectly in the Brooklyn he had grown up in. The point had been to show people, especially a date, that you had a good job. But things were different now. What was it that had occurred to him earlier? Oh, yeah. *Hip done in the right way and with the right people meant money...*

He took off his jacket, his white shirt reflecting the sun, ready for his transformation. New Brooklyn, here I come.

Coffee, like the ocean, was one of God's great creations.

CHAPTER THREE

Nicole Di Gioia's painting studio was a mess. In spite of her nearly all-night marathon of cleaning and rearranging, the space was no more people-ready than it had been the day before. Granted, her paintings and etchings were no longer flung here or there or propped sideways against the wall, and she had hammered in new nails in preparation for hanging several of her most recent creations. But the overall effect was still one of creative chaos.

Bottles of turpentine and filthy rags were crammed onto a cart, next to tin coffee cans holding paintbrushes coated with what looked like years of dried and hardened paint. Photos, postcards, and other sources of inspiration were tacked up seemingly at random. Books on painting, architecture, and art history leaned crazily towards each other on out-of-reach shelves, and vinyl records near a turntable spilled out of their jackets onto the dusty floor.

One flight down from the studio, in the one room where she lived (and which spanned the entire width and length of the house), Nicole stretched hugely and breathed in the aroma of coffee freshly brewing on the stove. As always, it was a welcome antidote to the fumes from the studio's solvents and paints. The milk, in a little dark blue enamel vessel with a long handle, was gently frothing like sea-foam at dawn. For Nicole and most of her artist friends, coffee, like the ocean, was one of God's great creations.

She considered whether to run down to the newly-opened patisserie on Sixth Avenue for a croissant. Despite her burgeoning anger at the continuing gentrification of her surroundings, and perfectly aware of the hypocrisy inherent in her patronage, she still found it hard to resist the lure of a place that sold one of the few things she really liked and could still afford.

Nicole, and other young people like her, found themselves part of a caste in development since the Reagan era, that could perhaps be dubbed the rich-poor: those for whom the consumption of such over-priced items as an "upscale" pastry or espresso, or this month's digital thingy upgrade, substituted for the loss of scores of previously attainable middle-class privileges. Their savings and assets were nonexistent, and their futures uncertain at best, but like gold chains and hyped sneakers, these little treats provided instant gratification and a false sense of belonging to a more affluent group. The fact that the world of their parents no longer existed in America was old news, but tastes of it were comforting, even in miniature.

She decided against it when she remembered that her ankle hurt like hell.

Park Slope — the only neighborhood in the world where not moving aside for a stroller was classified as a hate crime. If so, she was technically guilty, but there had been two of them, like something right out of a single Brooklynite's fitful nightmare, two *double* strollers aimed right at her, and so there had really been no place to go. Just before the collision, she had seen the steely glare of the woman with the blonde ponytail who had rammed her ankle as if to punish her for her unintentional defiance. If ever there was an argument against having children, thought Nicole, rubbing the bruise, it was the mind-blowingly selfish behavior of the colonizing white breeders.

Be that as it may, it was time to get started with her day. She limped to the stove, prepared her café con leché, retired to the table she had bought at a restaurant supply store in Chinatown, and tried to recall her actual accomplishments of the night before:

#1. She had successfully removed most of the belongings of the band her rock critic boyfriend was currently busy dissecting/analyzing/trying to manage. Various members of the Little Weevils – there were six of them - had been found sleeping in her studio one too many times. Since they had come under Ned's wing, she had gone upstairs to paint only to find the three or four of them who were invariably homeless camped out under an easel snoring or in a corner rolled up in the canvas meant for her next painting. With the Weevils just about to leave on a tour, and her studio open house immanent, it was the perfect time to effectively evict them by dumping their stuff in the trash.

The band had been formed by the disenchanted drummer of a rising thrash metal band who found himself bored to death by their visits to the MTV studios, and longed for the days of playing Deep Purple and Led Zeppelin covers in small, airless clubs. Fredericke had peopled his new band with members who looked remarkably like himself: small and short, with long flowing hair and longer pointed beards.

Their debris included sleeping bags not cleaned since the Weevil tour in Holland a year and a half ago, various drug paraphernalia, and piles of plaid shirts so dirty, so truly foul, that it was best to skirt them widely in order to avoid the new and unknown forms of life incubating in the filth.

#2. She had borrowed a ladder from the lesbians downstairs and had managed to fix, or at least temporarily seal off, the ever-widening cracks around the perimeter of the skylight. Sometimes the rain came in and sometimes it didn't, but it was clear that unless action was taken soon, the increasingly tropical New York weather would at some point turn the leak into a flood that couldn't be stopped. Murphy's Law said that if she didn't do anything, the torrent would begin just as soon as her invitees had congregated in her studio.

Sally, the sixtyish butch gay woman who owned the building, was nice enough, even willing, in her younger days, to take a hammer or a drill to a problem on short notice. But her partying, motorcycle-riding days had finally caught up with her, and the sight of her clad in her work overalls, bravely dragging her toolbox and panting halfway up the stairs made Nicole feel guilty.

So she'd applied the sealant herself, and now she was ready and, she reflected, a bit superstitiously, just by that simple action, most likely even over-prepared. It was something she'd sworn long ago never to do again – to put too much effort into something that ultimately didn't matter. Most likely no collectors or gallery owners would show, and her hard work would just be a sign between her and God that as usual, she cared too much. But Lorelei had persuaded her to send out postcards, declaring that Mercury was no longer in retrograde and it was "the perfect time to make an effort to move forward in stalled and stagnant areas." If only for the sake of their friendship, Nicole had given in, waiting until the last minute to mail the announcements as if waving a defiant finger at the New York art world, or herself, she wasn't sure which.

#3. The third result of last night's preparation had been something she had not anticipated. It was when she was atop the ladder, applying the final coat of sealant, that she had looked down, and from her vantage point become aware that a theme could be seen emerging from the ten or twelve paintings that were no longer lying face down on the floor. Her pictures of the last several months had featured gigantic fat kittens squeezed between Manhattan's high rise buildings. Above them, enormous black pigeons roosted, squatting atop various icons of the New York skyline. She had added the final touch by flinging arcs of resin-treated authentic New York pigeon shit onto them ala the elephant dung on the black Madonna that had caused such a sensation in the aptly named show at the Brooklyn Museum.

Previous to this expression, she had gone through a phase of making Keane-like paintings of a battered Statue of Liberty, large eyes ever larger and a single tear rolling down the symbol of freedom's face. She had been painting to PJ Harvey, but abuse art was so 1993, and this was dangerously close, so when a splatter of avian feces had fallen through one of the cracks in the skylight right onto the picture, turning the painted tear into dripping excrement, she had seized upon it as a heaven sent tool that seemed to exactly match her current feelings.

What with all the cool women and artists that she had come to know over the years pushed out of Brooklyn so far that most of them were now living in other states, and the voices of dissent commodified, she had reached a point where the money, consumption and conformity of her environment could only be symbolized in one way.

There was only so much shit one city could take.

Nicole went up the stairs to the studio, put the first Clash album on the turntable and decided to have a fourth cup of coffee.

Buzz's afternoon wasn't going as well as he felt he deserved. The cock fest marathon he had enjoyed last night and into this morning had already faded from his mind, and the steady flow of pleasures and acquisitions he was used to had been interrupted by a nasty surprise. If his bank statement could be believed, he had managed to exceed his annual trust fund withdrawal limit only five months into the year.

Down the hall from his office he could hear his father's current angry outburst, and even though he was more than accustomed to Harry's tirades, the distraction only increased his ire.

He got up and slammed the door shut. What the fuck?? The bank must have fucked up, or Doug Holmes, his private banker, had fucked up. He was number one on Buzz's speed dial so Buzz called him immediately, leaning forward impatiently in his twelve hundred dollar chair, but to his outrage he got a message saying to call Doug at his Cayman Islands number. The cocksucker! Buzz didn't have it on speed dial and the idea of the delay that its location would entail was too much for him to bear. Doug's failure to answer the phone meant a fly in the ointment of the instantaneous relief that Buzz always expected: it was intolerable.

"Doug, it's Buzz." He was leaving a message on this number whether Doug liked it or not. "What the fuck?? I'm out of money?? Fucking call me."

An almost physical sensation of alarm was spreading throughout his body. Had his father finally managed to find the legal loophole that would allow him to pull the plug on Buzz's spending? His mother had set up the trust, and what he did with it was nobody's fucking business, he told himself. Ten or eleven nights out in the last two weeks at a cost of several hundred dollars each time - that of course didn't include the cash he'd laid out for drugs. The initial payments on the custom Hummer he'd already tired of, followed by his trip to Iceland, which had replaced the Pines in Fire Island eons ago as a cruising ground, his monthly rent of thirty-eight hundred dollars for his shitty apartment in Chelsea, the usual designer clothing must-haves. Nothing new... so where was the fucking money?

Had his father been spying on him? It was nobody's business, except of course when he violated the stipulations governing his conduct that his father had pressured his mother into adding on to the terms of the trust. They were still extremely lax, but with his ever-increasing addictions to drugs and sex, he knew he'd stepped over the line. Was Harry's shithead lawyer even now putting together a list of Buzz's 'activities'?

Luckily he had two other accounts that Harry knew nothing about. He had his own deals on the side, real estate and otherwise. The joke was on his father, who thought he was nothing more than a sponging, spoiled child. In fact (and at this thought Buzz's eyes glittered), on a number of occasions it was Buzz's unseen hand that had contributed to Harry's travails. There had been several instances where the balance had been tipped for or against Harry's plans by money passed between Buzz and interested parties.

Still, even those accounts were languishing and overdue for another infusion. Until that fuckhead Doug found out what had gone wrong, he'd need to keep his eyes peeled for opportunities.

A still-employed relic from the past, a church bell from one of Park Slope's numerous places of worship, had begun to chime. It was three o'clock. Do you know where your children are?

Harry was foaming at the mouth to anyone who would listen, and at that moment it was the largest of the three colossal bulldogs that he owned and that accompanied him to the office each day. Usually, they lay in state under and around his massive desk, immobile except for the constant panting and gasping for air that was their unhappy inheritance.

"Can you fucking believe it?" He was brandishing a copy of the Park Slope Herald as he paced up and down. "Do these jackasses think this is funny?"

Humphrey wrinkled his brow more than it was already wrinkled in an effort to understand.

Harry threw the paper onto his desk. The offending headline read "CHEER-O'S FOR ZEROES HEROES." Apparently vandals – terrorists, was how Harry preferred to think of them – had broken into several real estate agencies on Seventh Avenue, and, leaving everything else untouched, had altered the prices of the properties advertised in the windows. Zeroes at the ends of numbers had been painted over, so that, for example, a duplex on the park that was being rented out for eighty-four hundred dollars was now being advertised as available for eight hundred and forty. A rental on Fifth Avenue was no longer twenty-eight hundred but two hundred and eighty, and you could buy a junior one bedroom on Sterling Place for fifty thousand instead of half a million, and so on.

The picture on the front of the paper showed a group of smiling people standing in front of one of the agencies that had been hit:

> As a whole, neighborhood residents have found much to like about the "new" rents. "This is the way it was when I was a kid," said Sal Frazuppi, fifty-eight, who grew up in the neighborhood. "Those were the days!" "It's more realistic, considering what me and my friends make," twenty-seven year old Lauren Zeibel added. "The duplex sounds sweet! I've got a good deal in East New York, but

it'd be awesome to live here since there are so many cool bars," agreed Brett Thayer, thirty-one.

"Heroes! How could anyone call these criminals heroes?" Harry railed at Bogie and Sir John, the oldest and second largest of the pack, who had painstakingly raised himself and was plodding heavily towards the water bowl.

Gone were the days in Hollywood when Harry had a secretary to scream at to get some big shot on the phone should a problem arise. Things were so much more complicated now. For one thing, you weren't even supposed to call them secretaries and an innocent hand up a skirt was no longer tolerated. They could even sue you and ruin your career! And then things were so much more convoluted in general, full of twists and turns, fraught with unseen dangers. It slowed you down, you had to be careful every second, there was no knowing who was who just by looking at them anymore, there were no informal agreements among men, everything had to be done on paper. So you worked alone and the worst thing about it was that without someone to yell at immediately he was in danger of losing his thunder.

Who could he talk to? Bogie, Sir John, and the female, Sophia, were looking up at him with more intelligence and friendliness in their questioning eyes than he had seen in the faces of most of his employees, especially the two idiot brokers whose desks faced the window. His son was useless, that was already established. What about that Jim, or Flynn, or whatever his name was? He seemed like a smart guy, a guy who could get things done. But where the hell was his call? He was supposed to be wrapping up negotiations.

It was at moments like these that Harry questioned his decision to leave the West Coast. The move had come after his failure to garner the necessary support for his pet project, a remake of *Gone with the Wind* with George Clooney playing the role of Rhett Butler. His stroke of genius had been his idea to replicate the nationwide search for a Scarlett that had been conducted for the original production. It was a time-tested move that boosted publicity sky-high while at the same time harmlessly playing on the heart-strings of talentless girls everywhere. He would ultimately hire a name of course. Who, he had no idea, because in truth he didn't believe there *were* any true female stars anymore. They were all to him. Still, Clooney would carry it, and maybe his pal Brad ₋ould play the wimpy fair-haired rival Ashley who Pitt might regard as a character with depth. But he had been too emotionally invested, people crucial to the project's support hadn't gotten on board, the marketing flaks had doomed it saying it was way too long for today's audiences as well as raising more red flags than the Confederate army in its potential to offend. It had been just the latest in a string of creative disappointments that had followed his early successes, and it was finally too much to bear. He was limping like a one-clawed crab half eaten by seagulls; to survive, he'd have to make his way to other, more stagnant tide pools such as advertising, but he refused to spend the rest of his life feeding snacks to the seals at the zoo, aka the clients and consumers, with their cries and thomping flippers and their perpetually unfillable appetites.

But now here he was again, facing the same, or worse. He was finally doing the right thing and making money the bottom line without regard to anything else and the goddamn papers were coming at it like a bevy of bikini-clad Hanoi Janes parachuting behind enemy lines, spewing propaganda and distracting the troops with the humor they flaunted like fantastic breasts. *Wait a minute... that wasn't half bad...*

But no, films were behind him, even though - and here he sat down again and leaned forward, nodding to himself in agreement at the comparison forming in his mind - those who opposed his developments here were just the same as those established actresses who, back in the good old days before the advent of the PC world, had been dubbed "difficult." Actually, that had been all those women who insisted on airing their views and opinions, but especially those who, like Barbra, had obstinately demanded actual input and decision-making power and then went even further than that by declaring their intention to direct, to the absolute horrification of the Hollywood honchos.

Yes, the old truisms were still true. In Hollywood, everyone was an actor who wanted to direct. In New York, everyone was a critic who had no intention of ever being anything else. It was apparent he would have to wrangle with the East Coast assholes too.

Sir John (named after Gielgud), had placed his chin on Harry's foot and was rudely displaced when his owner grabbed the phone with a new burst of energy. Harry dialed The Herald and barked out the name of the Editor-In-Chief.

"Dan. Harry Harmony, Harmony Realtors."

"Hello, Harry." They had met a couple of times at various political functions, shaking hands and filing each other's name away for future reference for attacks or favors.

"Everything good? What's going on?" said Harry. He scanned the article in front of him again.

"You read the papers Harry, right? You know as much as I do."

Okay, the waters were cold. That wouldn't stop him from plunging in.

"Dan, what's this 'Zeroes Heroes' thing headline? You know what I'm talking about. Come on, you want to go back to the Seventies? You want Willard IV filming in Brooklyn without a set? You got gay coffee on every block now! What, you wanna buy crack instead?"

"Harry?"

"Yeah?"

"It rhymed."

"What?"

"The headline. It rhymed. It sells papers. How about this? You do your job and I'll do mine."

"Oh. Sure." Harry paused, unsure what to say next. "You going to the Leukemia Fundraiser?"

"I'll be there, Harry."

"See you then."

"Right."

Harry put down the phone, leaned back, looked up at the ceiling and sighed at the same time that Sophia passed a long, odorous, gaseous cloud.

Uncomfortable in his chair that was every day feeling tighter, he drifted off into a nightmare-ridden nap where streams of Brooklyn residents had turned into zombies and were staggering down the streets, punching their way through the doors and walls and smashing windows in William May and Corcoran looking for deals, their wild eyes and rigid bodies refusing to take no for an answer.

Flynn's foray into the land of sartorial splendor was turning out a bit differently than he had anticipated. From the moment he had entered the store he had felt like a fish out of water. He wasn't sure whether he had imagined it, but it seemed to him that his very entry had caused consternation among the staff. Was it because his conservative attire identified him as someone who did not belong?

As he meandered around the store and inspected several price tags in disbelief (the cheapest item of clothing, a brown T-shirt with red crisscrossed lines, was forty-six dollars), he could have sworn he was being followed. A young African-American man, wearing one of the aforementioned T-shirts, as well as two square-shaped studs in his ears that appeared to be diamonds, kept appearing at the rack next to wherever it was that Flynn was browsing.

Flynn examined a pair of pants with a three-hundred dollar tag. Did they think he was going to steal something? The thought was distressing and quite new to him. It was true that a close scrutiny of his suit would reveal that it was becoming a bit scruffy – he had noticed this morning that he had been treading on the cuffs of his pants in the back and they had become a tad frayed and dirty– but surely, that couldn't be reason enough to single him out.

Just because he was different...and did they think, or rather, however did they *know* that he couldn't afford to shop here. For all they knew, he told himself in an effort to counter the virgin hurt, he could be a rap star who just happened to be wearing a suit that day.

Well, to hell with them, he thought, and made for the door. The young man and a girl cashier with a page-boy haircut and plaid miniskirt now appeared to be in some sort of conference. Was it about him, he wondered, with increasing paranoia?

As he neared the door he felt a hand on his shoulder.

"Hey."

For some reason, he jumped guiltily. Shit! Why ever would he do *that*? He hadn't done anything!

"Hey," said Flynn, turning around to the sight of Mr. Diamonds.

"You look like you could use some help."

What the hell did *that* mean?

But in the ensuing moments, to his surprise, he found a friend. Trevor, as he introduced himself to Flynn, listened politely as Flynn, in an effort to justify his presence (although why he felt he had to do *that*, he had no idea), admitted that he had come in looking for something "trendy". "For an important meeting," he explained, "but in Brooklyn, not Manhattan," he had continued, feeling ever more ridiculous. But Trevor only nodded soberly as he took in the information. Not only that, but, further encouraged by Trevor's helpful and friendly demeanor, Flynn finally came clean about his limited budget, wondering, at the same time, why it was he felt compelled to do so and why he felt like he was visiting the father confessor.

Trevor led Flynn back into the store, where, after further discussion aided by the comments of Deni, the mini-skirt clad "girl" who turned out to be a boy, it was determined that perhaps, due to his limited budget, "accessorizing" rather than buying an outfit might be Flynn's best bet.

Trevor selected a shoulder bag in a rich brown with an indecipherable yellow pattern. At first Flynn resisted, even recoiled, at the thought of marrying his grey conservative suit with something so, well, casual was the kindest word he could come up with, but Trevor and Deni insisted that the combination definitely "worked."

"A lot of the guys do that," Trevor said. "Matter of fact, Busta Rhymes was just in here the other day, he bought six of them."

Flynn had not the slightest idea who or what "Busta Rhymes" was, but was struck by their reverent looks. Feeling cornered but at the same time hopeful, he gave in.

"When you have that meeting," added Trevor, "everybody's gonna notice this bag. That's what you want if you want them to let you in the game."

Deni adjusted the strap of the bag in a diagonal sweep across Flynn's chest, fixing it with exquisite care as if it were a Miss America banner, then stood back and surveyed his handiwork. Then, as if following a flash of genius, he leapt to the counter and grabbed a pair of tinted glasses from a rotating stand. He slid them onto Flynn's face, leaned forward and flipped just the tiniest little bit of Flynn's hair down over one eye.

"There. Now you look just like Allen, the art dealer I used to date." He pursed his lips into a small satisfied smile that contained an odd combination of lust and loathing.

"Keep them," he hissed, and Trevor pretended to look elsewhere as Deni took Flynn's payment for just the bag.

Flynn accepted the glasses, surprising himself with the way he nodded at Deni in thanks without missing a beat and the lack of guilt he felt about taking the stolen gift. After all, didn't he deserve these things as much as anyone? And why not appear to be an art dealer? Real estate agents were hardly known for their fashion sense. Already, standing outside the door, Flynn thought he saw a fresh interest in the faces of the people who slouched by him with their own accessories, technological and canine.

It seemed like a contradiction, he thought, but if standing out was a way of fitting in, as Trevor had seemed to imply, this was surely a good beginning.

If one could judge by Barnaby's reaction, Flynn's new look was definitely making an impact. Usually around the younger man he felt ghostlike, one could almost call it invisible. Barnaby's serious stares for the most part lacked any decipherable emotion. Occasionally, when considering something he judged less than intelligent, disapproval would register in his eyes, but it never stayed there long, and it was never accompanied by surprise or disappointment. His asceticism in emotional display matched his dress and eating habits, so Flynn was unprepared for any form of feeling appearing on his roommate's face.

"Yo," said Barnaby, looking up from his book of Truffaut interviews with Hitchcock, and staring at Flynn, breaking his usual code of silence. Generally, unless Flynn spoke first, it was likely that there would be no conversation at all, not even a quick hello. He didn't really take it personally, that was the way a lot of guys were, after all, but for someone who had grown up in a part of Brooklyn where one could still rely on a friendly acknowledgment from almost everybody, it took some getting used to.

"Hey," said Flynn.

A pale shadow of perplexity passed for a millisecond across the production assistant's face. Flynn waited for the disapproval that would surely follow.

"That's cool," said Barnaby, nodding at Flynn's bag.

Flynn's eyes widened in surprise.

"Really?" Flynn glanced down at the brown canvas covered with yellow squiggles that rested against the gray of his pants.

Barnaby nodded again. "That's like…dead elephants."

"What?"

"I can see them. Right on."

Flynn stared at his bag in alarm. What the fuck had he gotten himself into this time? Had he totally missed something? But he didn't see anything beyond the yellow scrawls, certainly not a poster for PETA.

"I don't see - " he began, but it was too late. Barnaby had returned his focus to intellects long departed.

Flynn smiled unsurely as he went to his room. The judgment at Nuremberg was over and he had been identified as being on the side of the guiltless. Trevor, Barnaby, that…Deni, and what was it…Buster? They were all in his court now, or maybe he was in theirs. Could it be that his embracing of the new was already proving worthwhile?

It was beginning to feel like the eighth hour. Nicole had discovered, to her disgust, that one of the Little Weevils, the smallest one, Fidel, had managed to evade yesterday's crackdown. He had stowed himself away in a cupboard meant for her oil paints and palettes, and she had nearly had a heart attack when she had come across him curled up in a ball and sleeping off the effects of copious amounts of alcohol. The smell of whiskey combined with paint fumes and the stench of his rag-like attire was so rank that she had the immediate instinct to call poison control. Instead she called Ned and began to yell at him in the manner of someone who has just found a giant rat in their apartment due to the irresponsibility of an absent roommate.

But Ned was in the middle of the fifth chapter of his Weevils' biography, and like an astronaut contacted by NASA administrators, responded in an arrhythmic cadence broken by lengthy gaps that let Nicole know his mind and eyes were fixed on something far away from her concerns: the Black Hole of the Laptop.

"That's… great…"

"Great? What the fuck, Ned? Get over here and get him out!"

"Right… who? Oh, Del. I need to talk to him about the…hold on…" Nicole could hear the furious tapping of the keyboard. "Okay. Yeah, here it is. The time the Weevils went to the transfusion facility in Switzerland to see where Keith Richards has his blood changed. I mean used to. Before Patti. Can you get him to call me?"

Nicole slammed down the phone. The workings of Ned's mind, once so fascinating to her, had increasingly lost their luster.

There was a disconnect, she had come to see, between his obsessive quest for verification of the most insignificant details of pop culture and his lackadaisical approach to follow-through in real life problems. There was a gaping contradiction in his non-action regarding the many and varied sleazy aspects of the music industry and his insistence on the "integrity" of the artists he championed, as if somehow the purity he imagined they possessed separated him or even raised him above the not-so-nice world he had chosen.

The religious zeal with which he catalogued the intimacies of other peoples' lives was also beginning to creep Nicole out. While there was virtually no progression in the emotional life of their relationship, he never missed a chance to minutely examine the making or breaking of his subjects' bonds.

But her disillusionment had truly burgeoned ever since Ned had begun to write the Weevils' story, tentatively titled "Against the Grain." She could see now that Ned aspired to be among the ranks of pop culture critics who were as responsible for creating the myth as they were for cataloguing it. She was shocked that he didn't see that his ambition was leading him out of the realm of true assessment and into the cesspool of marketing.

In many ways they owed their involvement to their shared awareness of this distinction. They had met at a party two years ago, and after exchanging a volley of barbed and cynical witticisms, spent the rest of the night on the roof drinking and spewing expletives about this very issue.

And now here he was busily sowing the seeds that would allow him to reap his own rich little harvest. Ned's current activities meant that the Weevils might just as well have been the newest manufactured pop sensation designed to milk the prepubescent pocket. Most annoyingly, it was obvious to Nicole that he still retained his "holier-than-thou" attitude toward what he considered "mainstream."

"Get out!" Nicole yelled at the diminutive band member while trying not to gag.

"Oh, hey Nicole," he said without opening his eyes. "Namaste. Band's coming to pick me up tomorrow a.m. Be out by then. Promise."

"You better be!" Nicole slammed the cupboard door shut. Ned really ought to call the bio "Dead Salmon." It was what Fidel smelled like and what the polluted mainstream always spawned.

There was still the question of the beverages to be figured out. In the past she'd always just run down and got the things she needed for a party or a date from the stores on her block, but since they'd all been shuttered, one by one, over the last year, her hunter-gathering endeavors had become that much more of a pain.

She missed those days. The best dinners she'd made for friends were just bottled beer from the deli and Kielbasa from the Polish grocery store. Then there were the birthday cakes from the Puerto Rican bakery: so sweet she almost couldn't eat them, but comforting in the way they reminded everyone of kids' parties when you stuck a couple of candles in them.

Now when she came home from her job at Porto Rico Coffee in the Village, the only thing she could do on her block was go get a drink at Aunt Muffin's. Which wasn't exactly what she wanted to do every afternoon. There wasn't even Mr. Valle at the shoe store anymore, who used to fix her heels for a dollar, and who'd insist she take a seat on a low stool covered with newspapers and who'd talk to her like a father in his strong Italian accent, occasionally embellishing his advice with gorgeous-sounding strings of his native language. Sometimes in the summer she'd come downstairs to get out of the heat in her apartment and sit in his air-conditioning and smell the leather of the shoes and handbags and he'd always make her smile no matter what. It would have been just rude not to have responded to his warm greetings in kind, and plus the way he worked so hard from morning til night and still was always so nice made her ashamed of the bitchy way she walked around complaining about everything. Even when he'd say "Where's-a you boyfriend? You don' have a boyfriend?" it never annoyed her like it might have if it had been someone else. She'd always say "sorta," because she felt like he was like the relative you wanted to have a good opinion of you and didn't want to tell about the loser in your life. In fact one time he'd seen her walking with Ned in his worn-out CMJ T-shirt from 1996 (the pride of his wardrobe) and torn brown corduroys, talking on his phone, ignoring her, intent upon some bit of business, and when she confessed to Mr. Valle that he was "kinda" the "sorta" guy, his response had been, "*he's-a you boyfriend? He no boyfriend for you!"* She didn't mind. In fact being able to acknowledge her questionable judgment in front of this kind old man was a huge relief. She could grin about it, and unlike it had been with her father, whose unpredictable rages had made her childhood and teenage years about avoiding him at all costs, the only thing that'd happen was he'd raise his eyes and hands to heaven in supplication that she do better.

Now, with all that gone, it was a true wasteland on her block. Like a beach boardwalk in the middle of winter. It was creepy. There was something grave-like about the dark empty insides of the stores. And even though she hadn't really known the people who lived in the other buildings well - the Puerto Rican teenagers who hung around outside the bodega every afternoon, the weary-looking Latino grandmother in her flowered day dress, the Chinese woman with her aged Chow - they'd exchanged hellos and small talk every day. She'd felt comfortable around them, anonymous and yet acknowledged in a way she liked.

She'd get Ned to bring the beer, she decided, rather than have to lug it all the way from the nearest supermarket chain. People might expect to have things to eat, but this wasn't a fucking Soho gallery show. *"I'm terribly sorry but I've run out of brie,"* she imagined herself saying. *"Would you care for some Key Food cheddar?"*

He would be late. Most likely, the Leather Extravaganza was already in full swing.

A strange thing had happened. He had lain down on his futon bed fully dressed, and closed his eyes, expecting that as usual, its obnoxious nature would prevent him from getting any rest. In this case though, he'd make it work in his favor, since all he wanted was a quiet minute to organize his battle plan. Almost as if to spite him, the futon seemed uncharacteristically to soften beneath him, with the result that when he opened his eyes again several hours had passed.

The apartment was deserted. Barnaby must have gone to a shoot. Flynn hurried into the bathroom and glanced at himself in the mirror as he relieved himself. His five o'clock shadow had turned into an eleven o'clock, but there'd be no time to shave.

Holy mother of shit! What had happened to him? When he was working for the bank he'd had to get to work at an ungodly hour, way before the market opened, and he'd never been late, but then of course those kind of lapses were simply not tolerated. He would have been fired immediately. You paid a price for getting paid. He ran a wet hand through his hair and hurried out of the apartment, almost forgetting his new shoulder-bag.

On Fifth Avenue, he slowed down his steps as he felt the cool breeze of the night. It was a Friday, and scores of people were out, in groups or, if alone, talking animatedly into their cell phones. The wide doors and windows of restaurants that opened onto the street, showed men and women canoodling at luxurious bars and couples on dates gazing at each other over tea lights. The scene felt surprisingly foreign to him now. He'd really only had a couple of beers at dive bars with Kev and Seth lately, for lack of anything better to do, and it had felt more like work than anything else. His dinners with his ex-fiancé Constance at the pricey and trendy restaurants of her choice seemed like they had happened eons ago.

He knew he had reached his destination when he was suddenly struck by the desolation. In contrast to the bright nightlife he had just witnessed, it was like suddenly finding yourself swimming in an ice cold patch of water in the middle of a warm lake. He hadn't noticed it so much in the daylight, but in the night, with its stores finally shuttered, the abandoned block all but disappeared into the darkness.

And from the outside, even knowing where it was, it was hard to find Aunt Muffin's. It seemed extraordinarily hidden for a place that had advertised a party. There were no red neon signs proclaiming "BAR" or "BISTRO" or anything else to welcome patrons, not even a crowd of the tourists who now flocked to the Slope on the weekends hopefully inspecting the premises for cachet. There was no velvet rope with a line of people hungry for the approval of the person who guarded the door, who was hungry for the surge of power that came with controlling a line of eighteen-year-olds with too-large plastic sunglasses.

Flynn approached warily and pulled open the door. He was immediately enveloped by a crush of bodies and the pounding of hip-hop music:

"Give it to me
Gimme that funk, that sweet, that nasty, that gushi stuff

But don't bullshit me
C'mon, gimme that funk, that sweet, that nasty, that gushi stuff"

"Ten dollars," yelled the woman standing just inside.

Flynn strained to hear her as he felt for his wallet.

"But it's sliding scale," she shouted.

"What?" Flynn yelled back.

"Sliding scale! If you can't pay it!" Flynn hesitated. At that moment he was whacked on his right side by a woman with a crew-cut wearing a black leather vest and an expression of laser-like intensity. Her knee was in between the thighs of a young Latina woman with dark hair, large gold hoops and a tight low-cut white shirt and as they danced they pressed into each other like mating cicadas.

Two girls both with long brown hair and matching jeans moved sensually along with the music as they held twin glasses of red wine precariously high above their heads and screamed sweet nothings or insults into each other's faces at close range. They were mere inches away from him and wine from one of the glasses sloshed over its rim and splattered red drops onto Flynn's bag.

And with the speed of someone preparing for a tackle, an invincible-looking African-American woman wearing a football shirt was pulling her pretty leather-mini-skirt clad partner by the hand out of the club, aiming directly at where Flynn was blocking the door.

It was clearly time to move.

Flynn grabbed five dollars from his wallet.

Would he have to show some proof of his eligibility for the reduced rate? He deserved a break, though, and since his two main money drains, his landlord and Starbucks, sure as hell weren't going to give it to him, he might as well get it here. No reason to feel guilty.

"I lost my job," he heard himself shout guiltily as he handed it over. It was true, after all. He had lost *a* job.

"Have fun!" the woman taking the money bellowed over the noise, giving Flynn an encouraging smile.

The club was wall-to-wall people and as he pushed forward into the sea of black leather jackets and wallet chains worn on the right side, and short skirts and little bags clutched under the arm at cleavage level, Flynn took in the fact that he seemed to be the only straight man in the club. *Was it cool that he was even in here at all?* He could see some guy couples that must obviously be gay, but not one brewski-swilling bro. Then what had given him entré? Had his magical shoulder bag gone one step beyond hipness and conferred upon him the coveted status of homosexuality?

Two women in motorcycle pants and jackets and army boots holding Budweisers parted to let him pass and he squeezed between them gratefully if a bit warily, giving them a nod and a smile that they didn't return.

He looked over at the bar, but he was separated from it by a sea of bodies. Not much chance for a beer here. But that wasn't the point of his visit anyway. It was all business.

Maybe he should just leave. But a sudden crush of bodies from behind shoved him deeper into the bowels of the club. Shit. He was going in.

He let himself be swept along, and was expelled from the mass moments later, landing in a small passageway by the bathrooms. A short, chubby, Puerto Rican girl with cropped hair, multiple piercings and a t-shirt with rainbow colors radiating out from its center stood in his way, banging on one of the doors.

"Fuckin' bitches!" she was yelling. "C'mon, mama, I got to PISS!" She saw Flynn and shook her head. "Melinda and Jen always in there *doin'* it. Damn, you'd think we'd have a bathroom for the staff!"

"You work here?"

"Yeah, but I got the day off. Jus' came to hang out, y'know. Meet some girlies. My girlfriend broke up with me."

"Oh, uh, bummer," he said.

"Yeah. She wants a house, kids, you know. I ain't ready for that."

The girl looked about seventeen to Flynn, but maybe he was wrong.

The door of the bathroom opened and the two women he had seen earlier drinking wine stumbled out, flushed and crying or laughing.

"Do you know where I can find the owner?" he said hurriedly.

"Sally? Oh, she in Provincetown. Hold on, I be right out."

Flynn mouthed a silent "*yes!*" to himself and raised his fist slightly in what he was not aware was originally a Black Power salute. There was a kind of serendipity in motion here, he mused. Him being allowed in, for one thing, and now meeting this girl, someone on the inside who just might provide him with the details he needed.

Moments later she re-emerged and smiled at Flynn as if they were old friends.

"I'm Wendy, by the way. You want a beer? Hold on, I'm gonna get us some beers."

It only took her seconds and she was behind the bar, giving a laugh and a wink to the two bartenders and rummaging under the counter. "Some" beers turned out to be six in total.

"You want to go out back?" she yelled over the noise, handing him his share.

"Sure!" Flynn yelled back.

Why was she being so nice to him? He didn't really have time to wonder as he followed her under an archway and further into the recesses of the club.

In the back room he almost dropped the bottles at the scene in front of him.

"I'm a slave for you - "

First he heard the song and then he saw the movie screen. An angular girl with a startling pixie face and short purple hair over one eye was slowly sliding the tip of a knife very lightly just below the collarbone and down into the cleavage of a girl whose features were also almost unbearably cute, and who was pressed up against a wall, oozing enjoyment.

Flynn stared at the film like an accident unfolding in front of him. Wasn't this stuff supposed to be, like, not okay?

"C'mon," shouted Wendy.

But Flynn stood rooted to the spot. He had wrenched his eyes away from the uncomfortable picture and was busy taking in the rest of the room: the women in leather thongs and bras who writhed on raised platforms; a group who held their beaming girlfriends on what appeared to be dog leashes; the pool table surrounded by female Budweiser drinkers in Full Leather Jacket, bent over and smacking their balls into holes while their competitors in mating styles prowled like wild animals behind them; the girls who watched them from the sidelines like groupies waiting to be chosen after the game. The college-age kids with newly cropped hair, low-slung pants and carefully chosen shirts from the boys department, standing in clusters of three or four, nervously chugging their beers and shyly scanning the room, while the brave among them advanced to stuff bills into the dancers' crotches with huge triumphant grins on their faces, for all the world appearing to Flynn exactly like freshmen at their first stripper/frat party.

Wendy had crossed the room and was standing by the door that led to the outside and Flynn shook himself out of his daze and remembered his purpose and what he stood to lose if he blew this opportunity to collect inside information.

But something else shocking to him slowed him down as he made his way through the space: he became aware that he was apparently invisible to the all of the girls, even the ones with short skirts and plunging cleavage. It was unnerving; he was used to being noticed right away by the opposite sex. He had to remind himself that it was the milieu, not him, that had caused the change.

He crossed in front of the oblivious women to the sound of the singer penning a love letter to the Marquis de Sade.

The patio had flagstones and picnic tables with benches. Flynn didn't see any leather-clad patrons here, just chummy-looking groups of mostly middle-aged women sitting around the tables talking vigorously. Lights had been strung around the surrounding wooden fence and a barbecue was in progress.

"Takes all kinds, right?" said Wendy, referring to the party room. "Not Sally though. She more like these dykes here. You want a burger or something?" They were enveloped by a cloud of pungent, herb-scented smoke. "We got tofu-dogs too."

A woman with big shoulders stood protectively over the grill.

"These are all taken," she barked. "And there are no more veggie-burgers!"

Wendy led a discomfited Flynn past the grill master. "Don't worry about her," she said. "She always flippin' out about somethin'." Flynn barely heard her. He was still recovering from hearing her use the "d" word, which he had always thought was as forbidden as the "n" word. *Maybe though when _they_ used it …*

They sat down and Wendy raised her beer for a toast.

"Salut," she said, giving him the same wide grin he had seen earlier.

Tree branches stretched over their heads, forming a leafy canopy. Wendy seemed very comfortable in her skin, Flynn noted. Her friendliness didn't seem at all fake or forced.

Flynn returned the toast. "So," he said, "how long have you worked here?"

"Like, two years? Yeah," she nodded. "'Cause me and Carmen just got together. I remember 'cause when I first told her I was workin' here she was like all on my jock. First she want all her friends to get in for free. Then she want me to ball her on the bar, too."

Jock? Ball? Flynn hoped the bewilderment didn't show on his face.

"I shoulda known right there it wasn't gonna work out. Man, she wanna get me in trouble? I'm just bussin'!" She took a long swig and burped without apology.

"So…Sally…you said she's out of town?"

"Ohhh---*mama! Mmmm.* Look!" Wendy tapped on Flynn's arm. "Yo, check her *out.*"

He swiveled 'round to see again the same young Latina woman who'd been held in the grip of her current or would-be lover when he'd come in the club.

"Um, I think she's taken." Flynn sat back and took a long swig of his beer. He was beginning to feel restless, but it was best he just chill. Earn her trust. Or rather, not lose it, since it appeared that she had already bestowed some measure of it on him for no apparent reason. The thing was to scope things out. Stay on the radar. Don't show he was a newbie like he'd done with Mrs. Haliburton. Be a chameleon. Fit in but stay out. His head was beginning to hurt with the barrage of sound bites he had to summon for the occasion.

"Oh, *shit.*" Wendy saw the object of her affection being trailed closely. "That fuckin' bitch Terry, she a total player. She fuck everything in here with a skirt. *Damn.* She psycho too."

Somehow Terry had felt eyes on her, and she turned coldly in their direction, catching Wendy's eye and holding it.

"*FUCK YOU*," Wendy said in a sing-song voice, but she kept her voice low.

"How come she went away?" said Flynn.

"Huh?"

"Sally? How come she went to Provincetown?"

"Oh, yeah." It started to rain but they were protected by the trees and an umbrella above the table. "Too much shit coming down. You know, with the block."

"Really?"

"Yeah. First this guy come around in his mad cool ride he like, oh, we could make a deal, you know, sell the building. But she don't wanna."

"How come?"

Wendy leaned forward and looked at Flynn.

"Sally like, old school, you know?"

Flynn didn't, but he nodded slowly and chose his words carefully.

"Of course. So she wanted it to be like…" He let his words trail off.

"You know, like, how it used to be. For the community, you know?'

Wendy paused. For just a moment doubt showed on her face.

"You a friend a hers, right?"

"Not exactly. I just…care what happens to the neighborhood."

"Oh. Okay. Anyways, so then she gets this call, right? Some guy like, hey, you don't want to make a deal with those guys, right? So she says who the fuck are you? I mean, she don't talk like that, she too nice. He says that don't matter but he can make things right.

"Anyways so I come in on a Monday, y'know, help clean up, 'cause Sundays we got L-Word and those bitches get *nasty*…so anyways, she's just sittin' there, in the backyard starin' at a wall and I'm like whoa, what's up. She started talkin' like how she's been here for thirty years and how she don't wanna go anywhere and I'm like hey, you could open up a club somewheres else, but she look at me like fuck no, then she say you don't understand. She goes like, back when I came out in the 50's forget it there was no place safe to go. So I'm like I know for a long time they didn't have anything in Queens and now they got Chica night on a Tuesday. So then she look at me like weird and she says, 'You girls talk about 'discrimination' *now?* You don't know what you're talking about. Back when *I* was comin' out, all we did was hide. It was a underground thing. It still is. You know how you know? 'Cause women still afraid.' She goes thas why I got property. Is supposed to be mine for *life*. Then she starts cryin' and I like totally freaked out 'cause I never see her do that before. I'm like hey mama, it's okay. She goes, 'they used to take us out and rape us. The cops.' "

Wendy sat back. "Whew, I could use a couple shots right now."

Flynn noticed he was gripping his beer so tightly that his knuckles showed white.

"Sure. What'll it be? No, no, it's on me."

He stood up and walked up the patio steps and back into the darkened room where the dancers and the music and the films were still going.

He had to pass uncomfortably close to a leashed girl and the woman who held her gave him a knowing grin.

"Hey. Nice strap. I like your bag."

It was going on 2 a.m. and Dale Shaw was in the process of being bored to tears. Literally. As she sat in the cozy confines of the Al Di La Wine Bar, which had been specially reserved for the entire week for the afterhours enjoyment of the cast of "The Slope Also Rises" and their rich and influential friends, and stared across the table at the CFO of a global media conglomerate, she found herself growing increasingly numb to his monologue. Even the heady aroma and the rich depths of the Shiraz failed to anesthetize her to the point where she could self-administer an artificial injection of interest, let alone desire. Still, the wine lay like a tiny lake of rubies in the crystal valley of her glass. It was a beautiful thing.

With the ease of a trained thespian, and without hearing a word he was saying, she let her face take on a variety of subtle expressions to match his: an amused glanced here, a look of concern there, a trademark raised eyebrow to mark what she instinctively sensed were his standout moments. What was so valuable about the latter technique was that it could be interpreted in so many ways – as a show of surprise, a question mark, a sophisticated way to display humorous appreciation, even an icy and controlled sympathetic or merciless outrage – and she employed it on and off set to convey all these, and more. At its essence, it showed that you were "getting it." Like monosodium glutamate, it enhanced the flavor of even the most tired dishes.

At this particular moment she decided that the sudden appearance of tears would be the quickest and simplest way to make her exit, as well as an always welcome chance to practice her skills. He was a powerful man and it wouldn't do her any good at all if he felt rejected.

She began to concentrate until a watery film obscured her vision.

"I'm sorry," she said, although he had noticed nothing.

She put her hand out across the table and laid it gently on his forearm, arresting the progress of a forkful of grilled sardines. Years of experience had taught her that it was supremely wise to make her escape before men like him made their first pass and discovered that she was not the available sex machine of their fantasies.

"It's the stress of the day, the long shoot…please don't take it personally," she said, letting just the hint of waterworks begin to well in her eyes. The trick was to give a sneak preview of what was to come and leave it at that. Once the deluge – real or conjured – had begun, most men felt obliged to show sympathy or offer support, maybe even ask for an explanation. But one and all, they invariably flinched from the tangle of invisible emotional ties, and it was at that precise moment that the avenue to freedom opened.

She rose to her feet.

"Take care," he said, not getting up, his mouth open and filled with partially chewed sardine.

Dale replied with a faint smile that held just a trace of longing and regret and glided towards the door. Perfect.

Outside, it was not as warm as it had been earlier. She felt the chill on her bare shoulders but her face felt hot and flushed, both from the wine and the close atmosphere of the party room. She could call her car or she could take the short stroll to the nouveau hotel where she was staying; it was an outpost of gentrification on an otherwise desolate street.

She began to walk. It would cool her down and help rid her, if only temporarily, of the professional exasperation that was becoming more and more difficult for her to contain as the weeks went by. She had really begun to fear that one of these days she would throw that glass of wine straight into Mr. CFO's face.

It wasn't just him. She crossed over from one avenue to the next, and paused on the corner. *Was her hotel to the right, or left?* She tried to recall the counsel she had received . Remember that "as the street numbers go up, you're going South." Huh? *So that meant...*he was a cliché, really, a stereotype whose behavior she would recognize in any movie as based on truths long since revealed and no longer surprising... *and what avenue was it on?* ...but added to the fact that her role in "The Slope Also Rises" was also redundant, a re-playing of the "Fatal Attraction" dynamic that was periodically offered up to the American nuclear family as a focus point for their ills, and that the series' male star was yet another balding past middle-aged actor accepted as eternally sexy while her age was always hanging over her head like an axe, and made turning down any role at all a gamble, she had the eerie feeling that the totality of her work world was itself beginning to resemble an amateurish film script.

One of the street lights was out and a van was driving slowly behind her. *Paparazzi here? How did they always find you?* Her ennui was oozing from her like ink from an octopus, and yet she was still visible to her would-be consumers. But she was a professional, always ready to slip into character in the blink of an eye, or a camera.

She stepped forward, flashed a smile and bared her best leg.

"And - *yo*." That was Barnaby-speak for "action." It was his turn to direct and he didn't give a fuck what verbal clichés the mainstream shitheads thought was sacrosanct. He and his film buddies were busting down the entrenched model of hierarchical authoritarianism in every way possible, and that included doing away with commands to his peers. At his words, the group of young men illegally filming by the canal went into, well, action.

IT CAME FROM THE GOWANUS
Act 1, Scene 1
EXT. GOWANUS CANAL – NIGHT (PRESENT DAY)
It is dark and desolate. The only light is a bright moon above. There are no houses nearby, only industrial buildings and a small empty, grassy lot that leads down to the water. A CANOE is tied up and floating a few

feet off the landing. We hear the sound of approaching footsteps and laughter.

ENTER HENRY AND CECE. They are both just out of college. Henry's tie is undone and his shirt is partially unbuttoned. CeCe is wearing a flimsy dress. They are obviously both very drunk.

CECE
(giggling)
Ooh! It's so dark down here! It's creepy!

Henry lopes down to the waters' edge.

HENRY
Wow. Look at this. A boat. We should go for a ride.

CECE
Ick! Are you serious?

Henry steps into the boat, which rocks violently from side to side.

HENRY
Whoa! Shit!

CeCe shrieks with laughter. Henry regains his balance, then bows down in an exaggeratedly gallant fashion and holds out his hand to CeCe.

HENRY
(In an Italian accent)
Please-a to take a ride on my gondola.

CeCe, smiling, takes his hand and half steps, half falls into the now wildly rocking boat. They collapse onto the bottom and into each others' arms.

CECE
I bet you say that to all the girls.

HENRY
Say what?

CECE
You know, ask them to ride on your...gondola.

Henry responds by starting to kiss her neck. He slowly slides his hand up towards her breast. We hear the loud sound of the water sloshing against the side of the boat.

CECE
Wait! What's that?

Henry continues what he is doing.

CECE
I heard something.

HENRY
(kissing her)
Yeah, it talks.

CECE
No, seriously.

She pushes Henry away and half sits up in the boat. Her dress is slipping off her shoulders, partially exposing her breasts.

HENRY
(reaching for her)
C'mon, baby. There's no one here.

CECE
(looking around her)
It was like – there was something in the water. Didn't you hear a splash or something?

HENRY
(annoyed)
It's water. It splashes.

CeCe spies a cooler behind them in the boat.

CECE
Hey, what's this?

Henry, frustrated, gives up on sex for the moment and props himself up
on his elbows.

CECE
Look, it's a cooler.
It's so heavy!

HENRY
Has God been merciful and granted me some brewskis?

CeCe pries open the top. She attempts to raise a heavy mesh sack.

CECE
Oysters??

She peers at a sticker on the cooler and reads:
"For a.m. delivery, Blue Ribbon Restaurant."

HENRY
(smirking)
You know what those are good for…all we need is a little champagne to
go with …
He pulls her back down towards him. They begin to kiss again. Suddenly
the boat starts to rock and shake wildly.

HENRY
Damn I'm good.

CECE
(screaming and looking up from below Henry)
Aahhhhhh!

HENRY
Hold on, wait for me.

We hear a monster-ish roar and see what CECE is looking at: THE CREATURE FROM THE GOWANUS, which has risen up out of the water and is towering over them. It roars again and lifts its monster-ish fins/talons out of the water and begins to claw at the boat. CeCe and Henry scream and cower back into the canoe.

HENRY
(in an anguished tone)
What does it want???

Doom appears imminent, as it lunges for them.

HENRY
Do you want her? Take her!! No problem, dude!

CECE
The oysters! I think it wants the oysters!

CeCe and Henry grab the sack and heft it together into the gaping jaws that are now mere inches away. The creature roars and thrashes, then disappears back into the water. Shaking, they pull themselves by the rope back to the landing dock, stumble out of the boat and collapse, shaking, on the ground.

HENRY
What – what was that???

CECE
(catching her breath)
I don't know… But whatever it was, it was hungry. Very, very, hungry.

CLOSE UP ON CECE'S FACE, EYES WIDE WITH TERROR.

Barnaby, looking through the camera, drew back his head and nodded in satisfaction. "*Right on*, sister," he said, "*Witness*. The money-hungry bastards are eating us alive. Oh, yeah," he called out. "End it. Whatever. You guys know."

    Buzz was ecstatic. His marathon of cruising was over. He had found The One. His throat was dry. He hadn't moved, barely blinked for hours for fear the object of his affection would slip away. If he closed his eyes he might find it was all a dream, the fulfillment he had always known was in store for him snatched from his gaping jaws by a fucked-up God:

THE DISCUS THROWER PENTHOUSE
Duplex Ultra-Full Service 3-Bedroom/3-Bathroom Corner
Unit/Bridge/City Swept
EXCLUSIVE!
This *Private* Penthouse Home (only 2 units on this 37th floor Aerie) features 2523 Sq. Ft. of Breathtaking North and East Birds Eye Views of the Empire State Building, several East River Bridges, Brooklyn, and Beyond. Sparkling, Brand New. Features a PRIVATE 5,000 Sq Ft ROOF PARK, Swimming Pool/Hot Tub, Squash Court, ½ Basketball Court, Gigantic 25' Ceilinged Health Club, Bowling Alley, Locker Rooms with Saunas, Yoga and Ballet Room, Business Center, and Screening Room. All with Full Service 24-Hour Doorman and Concierge. WALL STREET JUST AROUND THE CORNER! FINANCIAL DISTRICT!! WON'T LAST!!!

    But there it was. He sat back from the computer screen and pushed away the head that was under his desk. Barely remembering to put away his package, he stood up and walked out onto the terrace of his Chelsea apartment.
    Why hadn't he noticed the stars before? There they were, dotting the celestial canopy, and it appeared to him suddenly as if the

Why hadn't he noticed the stars before?

constellations themselves formed the New York skyline, as if even the cosmos echoed this burgeoning new romance. He was in love.

Striding back inside he fixed himself a drink. It had slipped his mind that he flipped apartments like he did sex partners, tiring of their charms almost immediately after the initial rush of acquisition had subsided. He always had at least two of his own personal properties either in the process of being sold or bought; they never became more than hotels for him, and that was why The Discus Thrower was perfect, because in essence, that was exactly what it was. Every need catered to, every want within easy reach…and that was another major perk, its proximity to Wall Street, with its on-the-down-low saunas and baths where businessmen in dark suits stripped next to each other in the lockers and took a load off during their fifteen hour days.

He heard a groan from beneath his furniture and remembered Tonio was down there.

That was the problem with submissives, they never knew when to give it a rest. Once he got the new place, the desk, along with its temporary occupant, would be left behind. He would no longer have time for games.

That piece of shit Doug Holmes had been sending him murky text messages from the Caymans – he would also have to go. Despite whatever financial mess he appeared to be in, one or two of his current properties put up to auction would cover the initial payment. He would hold on to at least one other apartment he had elsewhere; just because you were making a commitment didn't mean you couldn't have backups at the ready, you'd have to be a dumb bitch not to.

Once or twice he had even been saved from a major fuck-over by addresses he hadn't even remembered he still had. There was that time two winters ago when the bottom he had been fucking over the course of a few months and who he'd thought was Mexican turned out to be from Colombia and the nephew of a major player in the Colombian drug cartel. Some "relatives" of his had shown up demanding an enormous amount of cash for the equally enormous amount of primo cocaine they had consumed during various hardcore orgies and the bottom had told Buzz had come from the millionaire daddy who "owned" him.

He had come close to the edge of the knife on that one; only the rapid liquidation of an Upper East Side one bedroom had saved him from god knows what fate.

But this new apartment would be perfect; it would bring him to a whole new level in terms of lifestyle. That was the great thing about being rich: no matter what was actually happening in your life, you could always give yourself a raise. As long as the money held out, the only kind of reality check you ever needed was the one you wrote to yourself to make the kind of reality you wanted. The problem of his dwindling liquid assets would still have to be solved, of course, and plus he would need deep fucking pockets to buy the kind of accoutrements that would match the elevated level of The Discus Thrower. But it would be worth it. There was even a frieze in the lobby that depicted the famous statue; it would be like coming home every night to the hottest trick in town.

Tonio was issuing another strangled animal cry under the desk. But Buzz had no desire for sex. An entirely new thought came to Buzz: maybe it was time he got an actual dog.

The deep blue velvet of Nicole's ankle-length dress was so dark it could have been black. It wouldn't show the dirt and grit from the gravel and tar on her roof. For lack of any alternative buffer, she was kneeling on its hem, trying to spread plastic garbage bags over the parts of her skylight that had let in the rain once again. It was dark up here too, so much so, that she had to feel with her fingers along the perimeter of the glass to try and detect the cracks that had betrayed her.

"Fuck it." Nicole stood up. She stopped herself just in time from wiping her hands on the front of her dress.

Murphy and his relentless Law, who came through for most artists much more reliably than pretty much anyone else, had arrived as predicted. It had rained, *of course*, and the rain had *of course* found its way through her earlier repairs, and had dripped onto the shit on the paintings and onto the head of the one art dealer who had shown up along with his unbelievably bitchy assistant who hung like a wallet chain on his left side. They had been looking at her paintings with interest until the resin began to liquefy and they had bounded down the stairs, gagging, trying to escape the stink of months-old pigeon crap that now was spreading its boldly placed splatter on the Chrysler Building onto the biggest cat in "Fat Cats #3."

She went back down and flung open the door of her studio to survey the damage. Just the few minutes away was enough to give her some perspective. It was even worse than she had thought.

Her friends had been by and there was ample anthropological evidence, from the Brooklyn Brewery bottles to the ashes and butts crushed into glass ashtrays and the floor. Despite the widespread aversion to smoking, she refused to deny someone the right to relax with a cigarette while they spouted whatever inane rant they might draw up from the insides of their being at that particular moment, or have the comfort of their self-medication while they stared off into space and inhabited publicly the invisible caves most of them spent their lives hiding in. Even though she could see chalky grey smudges on the gold pillows of the three-legged couch she had hauled up the stairs by herself three years ago after finding it on the street.

At the last moment she had freaked out about not having any food for them, and so had run down to see what she still could get in the neighborhood, but all the new stores were too expensive so she'd opted for cheap Chianti instead. As it turned out, only the art dealer had had any, and his half-finished glass had been hastily abandoned on top of a pile of her prints, leaving red stains and another "natural" pigment in her work.

Ned was long ago gone back to "Avenue E," as he liked to call his neighborhood in Manhattan, which by the way infuriated Nicole, a native New Yorker who had grown up on the Lower East Side. The days of his crashing at her place most nights had passed. His apartment was now the locus of the "Weevils' business" which he cultivated with such dedication, and Nicole had not been sorry to see him go, she in fact welcomed it, she preferred her coffee in the morning without him now; two or three cups gave her more of a rush and a feeling of contentment than waking up next to him had in ages. His one track mind, his stinking corduroys, his new corporate being wrapped up in the tortilla of ambition and served on a platter with "alternative" sides! She was, to say the least, "over it."

It would have been nice, however, to have someone to help her in the task that could not wait: the casting off of her dripping, ruined artwork. Ned would have passed out anyway after his sixth beer. She'd do it herself, as usual. Why wait for help that would never come?

By the time Flynn stumbled out of the club in the early hours of the morning he had learned four very important things:

1. According to Wendy, no one knew when Sally would return, and it was anyone's guess what decision she would make about the building when she did.

2. The song "Hustler" by Jay–Z had a great beat.

3. It was easier to lie than he'd previously been aware of, or at least to skirt the truth, in pursuit of your goal. For example, telling Wendy he "cared" about what happened to the neighborhood wasn't technically untrue. It depended on what you thought of when you heard the word "care."

4. Someone other than Harmony Realtors was trying to get his hands on the Aunt Muffin's building.

Well done, he thought. A job he could be proud of. A bit of espionage here, a bit of camouflage there – it had been a long time since he'd had a feeling of accomplishment. Plus, his good fortune had continued: on his unsteady way to the bathroom he'd passed by a bulletin board where what Wendy consistently referred to as "the community's" attitude towards the development was made plain. An attempt was being made to form a committee to plan rallies and distribute leaflets against the project. What a bit of luck! He could report on this to Harry, plus, seeing it might have saved his ass. While relieving himself, Flynn had realized that he should probably cement his cover one way or the other, and so when he went back outside he'd headed off any questions by Wendy about who he was by hijacking the kilted gender-indefinable Deni's vision and mentioning casually that he was an art dealer (deciding at the last second not to call himself Allen).

The rest of his time with Wendy had been spent dodging the intermittent streams of water that poured off the side of the umbrella above them and listening to Wendy's tales of coming out (in kindergarten) and her recounting of the numerous volatile incidents that had characterized her relationship with her recent ex-girlfriend (drunken reunions and break-ups, fights over other ex-lovers, public declarations of love, promises to never forgive followed by deep tonguing, things hurled in the kitchen, stalking, etc).

On Monday he would arrive at Harmony bright and early, where he would surprise and gratify Harry by presenting him with the superior results of his undercover investigation. Harry would be re-affirmed in his choice of Flynn as the vital agent to carry out this crucial mission, and better yet, the new intelligence that there was another interested party would be a coup that Harry's son couldn't possibly match. The guy in the "mad cool ride" who had made Sally an offer and been rejected had almost certainly been Buzz, but whoever had offered to "make it right" for Sally, whatever that meant, must so far have remained undetected. If Harry had known, then getting rid of the competition would have already been part of the plan. For the success of the development, Harry would first have to get them out of the way. *We* would first have to get them out of the way, Flynn corrected himself.

Then on to do whatever it took to clear the building. All in a day's work. You gotta do what you gotta do. The phrases that popped into his head weren't ones he'd used before, but somehow they felt right.

It was odd, though. Flynn leaned against the side of the building down a few feet from the club's door. He drew a deep breath and looked up at the sky. At the same time, it was like he'd been exposed to things he didn't want to know, made uneasy by too much information that wasn't relevant to the task at hand. In that respect, he almost wished he hadn't met Wendy. It was too late now, though, he knew about the girls and their lives, the inner tangle of the owner's refusal with its ugly center, even been swept into the high-spirited crowd as it danced along to the repeated sing-along renditions of "I Will Survive" and Barry White songs that had replaced the dancers as the entertainment as the night went on. He had been confronted by a variety of happy, even joyous faces, beaming at him at close range, grabbing his hands, welcoming him into their midst. Even now he could hear the sound of the women laughing and chanting together in a chorus, bleeding out into the street:

> *Deeper and deeper*
> *In love with you I'm falling*
> *Sweeter and sweeter*
> *Your tender words of love keep calling*

Eager and eager, yeah
To feel your lips upon my face
Please her and please her
Any time or any place

I'm gonna love you, love you, love you just a little more, baby
I'm gonna need you, need you, need you every day
I'm gonna want you, want you, want you in every way...

Then the bass line came rolling out along with some "whooos" and more laughter.

Flynn shook his head to clear it and through the remains of his high remembered that it had been hours since he had checked his cell. He drew it out and scrolled through his texts and messages with the air of casual insouciance he had observed in others and imitated until it became his own, but in this case the fashion of the day did not serve him well. The device slipped from his languid hand and hit the pavement with an unpleasant whack.

"Shit." Flynn bent down to retrieve it and swept his hand over the pavement in the dim light and as he did so he felt something cool and smooth to the touch and because he was still a bit drunk he picked it up. Just some ad on a postcard. He was about to toss it back down when without warning a figure launched itself out of the doorway next to him, right into the light of the 1970's-era street lamp that was flashing on and off above him like a dying strobe at a down-at-the-heels disco.

He jumped. She didn't.

The sequins around the top of her dress were blinding. When his eyes recovered and he looked at her he noticed with a shock that it was the same dark hair swinging around the same very attractive face of the girl he had seen sitting on the fire escape. He felt a momentary panic, as if he had somehow just now been caught watching her.

As for her, her glance flitted over him with the speed of a practiced navigator of New York City streets, noting at first that despite his pretentious eyeglasses and bag, he was almost unnervingly handsome (that is to say, he was the type of guy she found wildly attractive and simultaneously decided would never be interested in her), then employing

He jumped. She didn't.

a millisecond pause in her analysis to imperceptibly select from her available options: full stop – almost never employed (even in the scariest moments it was best to keep moving); yield – if it was an old or disabled person or a female person of color (props to their growing power); green light – seize the right of way and ignore or walk straight into the older white-guy-in-business-suit who was moving for all the world like he was the only person *in* the world, although this animal had largely become extinct in New York, whether from a generational shift or backlash terror, to be replaced by the ubiquitous stroller moms with the exact same attitude. These latter species were sanctified by a rapidly eroding deference to the sacred institution of mother and child – for them, the yellow light between green and red was always on, signaling "you will feel anxious and increasingly pissed off, but you must do nothing."

Flynn had qualified for none of these special considerations, so she continued her advance to the gutter, dragging behind her several huge exploding-at-the-seams black plastic garbage bags. She had come out to dispose of her ruined artwork and get the hell out of her studio before she went completely crazy and by the way this was her turf so she would not alter her behavior one bit just because of his presence. She flung them into the street, then crossed her arms defensively and glared down at the sidewalk.

Flynn stood uncertainly, realizing that to resume groping along the ground for his phone might appear strange, especially since she was practically standing right next to him. Being raised in Brooklyn, he finally ventured a greeting. Having grown up in Manhattan, she fully cased him once more (phase two of sidewalk encounters – possible only after the initial determination that an obvious gaze would not get you blown away), and her eyes lit upon the card he'd picked up off the sidewalk.

"Oh!" she said, recognizing it as the invitation she'd sent out. "You're here for my show?!" She paused, waiting for him to reply. When he didn't, she chalked it up to New York City art world narcissism. "Oh, well," she continued, as he stood there, frozen, "thanks for coming!"

"Just thought I'd –take a look!" Flynn cut in awkwardly. He waved the postcard in the air. And now the paralysis was in her court. As she stood there smiling she remembered that she had just thrown out the majority of her soggy, shit-soaked paintings.

"Well, great!"

"I - dropped my cell," he said.

In the moments it took for him to retrieve it Nicole realized that she had no choice but to let him come up. Better that he bolted afterwards and berated himself for taking a chance, in Brooklyn and on a woman no less.

He'd have no choice but to go up. Flynn followed behind the train of Nicole's deep blue gown, taking in the once magnificent plaster moldings and wood wainscoting of the nineteenth century building, and tried not to stare at her ass.

What Nicole saw when she pushed open the studio door with Flynn beside her and apprehensively imagined she was seeing it with his eyes, was everything that wasn't there and "should" have been: piles of food for consumption; abundant drinks; the display of pricey accoutrements and gizmos currently de rigueur among Brooklyn artists, constantly streaming vital yet trivial data on a reproduction of a vintage industrial desk purchased for a thousand dollars on Atlantic Avenue; inscrutable app-loaded masculine-appearing max-information flow tool(s); eye-catching unidentifiable furniture; art/pop culture magazines; palm cards for other suitably hip au courant events; lighting; and people. People with various hats and shoes. A male with a particular hat digitally documenting wearing a poker face and loose expensive clothes. In short, a mix in and of itself an installation. A familiar, instantly recognizable place, not besmirched by unpleasant poverty and want. A Starbucks of a studio.

What Flynn saw was what looked like a bombed-out palace. High ceilings sheltered pieces of fallen and broken splendor: salvaged majestic armchairs with missing cushions; sweeping hangings of velvet and silk covering the windows; the faded gold of a chaise leaning to one side. Old books covered with dust, the faded elegant lettering of their titles still visible. Paintings propped up against the side of the walls as if they'd just been rescued.

Along with all this there were piles of paint brushes, tools, and scrolls of paper and canvas everywhere, and most oddly, a makeshift clothesline weighed down with what appeared to be dripping pictures.

Nicole hesitated on the threshold. She was aware that there were recognized ways one dealt with those in the "business." She too had read the varied tales of surprise successes borne of the special bonding between artist and rep. "There was that moment when I saw his work, " "he completely understood what I was doing," etc., that appeared in art magazines after the artist had been lifted out of his own special hell into the light by his gallery angel. Most of them involved a talent for self-promotion that was completely incomprehensible to her. There must be a script somewhere telling the artist exactly what lines to say to breach the mythic divide and bid adieu to Hades forever. She really should have read that handbook, or at least the Cliff notes. Instead, she turned to Flynn and said, "Welcome to my nightmare. Chianti?"

"What happened?"

The words were out of Flynn's mouth before he had even thought about them. *Damn.* Maybe this was the way art studios in general looked, and he was just too ignorant to know.

"The skylight leaked. I tried to fix it but…so much for that!" She shrugged. "I fucked it up, as usual!" She walked across the room, stepping directly on the artwork on the floor, making tearing and crunching sounds. "So…what gallery did you say you were from?"

"Uh, I didn't. It's, uh…" Flynn thought frantically. "The, uh…Brooklyn?"

"What? Wait. Is it *in* Brooklyn or is it *called* Brooklyn?"

"Oh, both." said Flynn, nodding vigorously. "We just thought – hey, this could work, you know, being in Brooklyn and then being called 'Brooklyn.' Because then, you just have to remember one thing."

It was all Nicole could do to keep her eyes from rolling upwards. She'd never heard of the gallery but then she'd left the postcards at various small stores in various "arty" neighborhoods where pretentious new spots were popping up overnight with the speed of pimples following a mayonnaise bender.

Flynn slowly circled the hanging paintings as Nicole poured wine into two chipped crystal goblets. He sniffed the air. Was it just him, or was there something a bit foul?

"I scraped most of the shit off."

"Excuse me?"

"The shit." Nicole held out his glass. "No one can say I don't use authentic New York materials."

Seeing his look of non-comprehension, she continued:

"Dung. Feces. Or to be more specific, pigeon crap. You know, like the Sensation show, the elephant shit? The Black Madonna?"

"Of course!" said Flynn.

"I was like, why shouldn't New York artists employ indigenous materials too?" Nicole plopped herself down on the unsteady gold velvet chaise. Thank God for Chianti. The Italians didn't fuck around when it came to having fun. Which was exactly what she was going to do, now that she had only one person to contend with. Dealer or not.

"These are…very interesting," said Flynn. He turned his head at various angles, hoping that would signify something.

"Fat Cats and Dirty Birds, Series 2. It's pretty much all I could salvage." Nicole knew it was a no-no to "explain" your art to a potential buyer, but she didn't care. "It's – you know, Wall Street. Predators, basically. Predators and Prey. Eaters and the Eaten. The Scum that is ruining our city and covering it with metaphorical shit. Maybe some of your clients?" Now she knew she had gone too far. Fuck it, who gave a shit. So to speak. Who wanted to sell to the corporate fucks anyway? Like they would buy her art that was all about hating them?

"What's wrong with the financial sector?" said Flynn, frowning.

"Everything," said Nicole.

"Really."

"Yup."

"You know," said Flynn turning to look at her. "There's be no New York City without it. Exactly how would that work? It's what keeps things running."

"For some people. For some people and their friends who want to take everything from everybody."

"Really?"

"Yeah, really." Nicole reclined fully, uncaring, on the wobbly couch, throwing caution to the winds as far as both her balance and her artistic career were concerned. Her sapphire gown clung to her body and her rhinestone teardrop earrings swung out from under her dark hair as she tossed her head for emphasis.

"Let me give you the perfect example," she said. "Developers. They've been trying to get us out of the building for months. You know, of all the heartless bastards in the universe, I have to say I think people in real estate are the worst. You spend years in a neighborhood, getting to know people, making it your home, maybe doing stuff to help spruce it up, and then, invariably, some son-of-a-bitch comes waltzing in and goes, 'This cake looks good. I think I'll eat it a piece of it. No, wait, I'll take the whole thing.' Eminent domain, aka Imminent Domination." The rant had been sprung like a happy rat from a trap.

Flynn looked down at his feet. "You sound – angry."

"No shit." Nicole couldn't stop her voice from bristling with well-deserved sarcasm. Unfortunately, at that exact moment the chaise shifted dramatically to one side and she rolled over and toppled to the floor.

"Great, Nicole," said Nicole.

"Are you okay?" said Flynn. He held out his hand as she struggled to get up amid her long dress and the spilled Chianti.

"I'm fine," she said. "I'll get up by myself."

A patter of rain began to hit the roof, then the steady plop, plop, of the leak in the skylight opening up began again.

"You should go," said Nicole.

Flynn looked up. "That needs to be fixed," he said.

"Yeah, I know. I tried to do it myself, but I fucked it up. As usual."

"Is there a way I could get up to the roof?"

Nicole stared at him. "Well, yeah," she said slowly. "There's a ladder."

"I'll go take a look," said Flynn. At the door he turned around and took off his tinted glasses. "I – can't really see too well in these," he said. His shoulder bag would get in the way too, so he left that as well.

Nicole watched his retreating back. *What the fuck? Why would he care?*

No wonder people didn't need gyms 100 years ago. Flynn pulled himself up the last metal rung and pushed open the trap door above him. Hunching over against the rain, he hurried to the bright square of skylight and squatted down to take a closer look. Not too bad. Growing up, he'd worked alongside his dad on the house, and helped out the neighbors too with various fix-its, especially the old women who were on their own. This wouldn't be a problem.

He sat back on his heels and then stood up, to be overwhelmed by the unexpectedly spectacular view of Manhattan. It was completely unobstructed and surprisingly close. The water of the river glistened like black ink and the gold and red lights outlined the castle-like panorama of the buildings.

"It's pretty, right?"

Flynn turned to see Nicole coming to stand next to him.

"It's a million dollar view," he said.

"I know. Don't remind me."

They stood together, watching the shimmer of the city, and then she looked up at him without his glasses and with his wet hair and he looked down at her, and just a hint of a regretful smile crept over both their faces.

When Flynn walked out of the building not long afterwards, the sky had just begun to lighten. But it was still too dark for him to see the long, low Lincoln Town car across the street that pulled slowly out and trailed behind him as he made his way down the block. He wouldn't have noticed, anyway. He was too busy whistling.

CHAPTER FOUR

Monday morning in Park Slope dawned bright and sunny. And it seemed particularly bright to Flynn, who had awoken feeling gifted with both a potential advance in his career and his new interest in the girl painter who would, partly through his own efforts, be forced to leave her home. That the two were at loggerheads was an uncomfortable truth that for the moment, at least, he preferred to put out of his mind.

On his way to the Harmony offices, Flynn made a stop off at the Rite Aid on Seventh Avenue to buy a notebook to record the information he'd gathered over the weekend.

The line to the one open cashier was unbearably long. People had piled their baskets full of tubes and bottles and enough bulk paper products to wipe the ass of the universe. Flynn found himself feeling more and more annoyed that he hadn't just gone to a stationary store to get this one thing, but then, he hadn't looked for one. In fact he didn't know if there *were* any in this area, and despite a fair number of experiences to the contrary, perpetually carried in his head the idea that chain stores were cheaper and would offer him more choice. And yet here was a perfect example of no choice at all. If he walked out in disgust he had no idea where else to go, and so he would have to wait and seethe as the weary African-American cashier unloaded each customer's plastic goods from their plastic baskets and piled them all into plastic bags, after running their plastic credit cards and asking if they had a plastic rewards card.

Using his "free" time to think ahead, Flynn ran over in his mind his next steps. Once liberated from these synthetic shackles, he would head on over to the next chain, where he would willingly extend his wrists to be encircled by the more comfortable mink-lined handcuffs of Starbucks. Then a quick stop at the bank chain to check his dwindling balance, where the rapidly blinking green lights of the available ATM's would raise his blood pressure and have him thanking god that he wasn't an epileptic. After that, his arrival at Harmony to impart the Good News that his fact-gathering operation had been successful.

On the line at Starbucks, Flynn meditated that the coffee would again be Grande. The self-imposed restraints of his relative poverty were beginning to imperceptibly loosen in anticipation of forthcoming rewards, due entirely to the new level of confidence his weekend work had provided. His serotonin levels rose and began to dance in the cosseted environment. As the server ran his credit card, he felt no fear, in fact he even cast a covetous eye on the gleaming attractively designed thermoses and the generously-sized porcelain coffee cups with their rich colors that were for sale. He stared at the deep blue of one of the cups for a while before it came to him that it reminded him of Nicole's eyes, and the thought flitted through his mind that it would be nice to buy one for her. They had agreed that he would return Thursday if it wasn't raining, and he was looking forward to it as if it was a date. But that would be weird, right? To show up with a gift? It was creepy anyway that he'd had to lie to her about who he was, and that he was ostensibly going to her house for the sole purpose of fixing her leaking roof. He hadn't even had the balls to ask her out. He'd make sure, he told himself, that he would keep his espionage work out of it, that he would go to see her again only because the image of her standing next to him on the roof wouldn't leave him.

With some effort he turned his attention back to his schedule for the day. Today there would be no desperate run to meet a client, no anxiety, he would use half-and-half in his Americano and buy a paper.

But his pleasant vision of urban heaven was not to be, for when he stepped outside, the news stand blared disturbing headlines from all three papers that were not *The New York Times*.

Forgotten coffee in one hand, he grabbed The Daily News:

TV STAR VANISHES

Dale Shaw, star of TV's "Open Heart Surgery" has disappeared in Brooklyn, and local police detectives fear the worst. Shaw vanished Friday night after a day spent filming her new series "The Slope Also Rises," in which she plays a seductive home-wrecker who sets her sights on a father of two who has moved next door with his young, pregnant wife. The 39-year-old actress was last seen leaving tony Fifth Avenue restaurant Al Di La at around 2:30 a.m. Questioned and released was J. Robert Shecnk, CFO of multi-media global conglomerate IAXX.

"She didn't order the sardines. That's all I know," Shecnk was quoted as saying, referring to the couple's tryst at the private party for cast and crew.

On a corner near the restaurant, fans gathered, leaving flowers and candles, and nearby residents expressed their concerns. "This is usually such a safe neighborhood," said Florence Rodgers, 62, despite the fact that muggings, thefts, and robbery are quite commonplace in Park Slope, according to the 78th Precinct police blotter. "Something like this just makes you worry about going out at night in New York."

Peyton Goldstein-Winnibrook, 27, who just moved to the Slope from Scarsdale, agreed. "It's totally safe around here. I just jogged through the park last night with my iPod and I didn't hear anything weird."

"My girlfriends and I walk home alone all the time after we've been out drinking all night," said Chattington "Chatty" Preston, a recent transplant from Connecticut, who asked that her age not be given. "What if I don't feel like taking a car?"

For now, police are canvassing the area and asking anyone who may have any information to call their local precinct or 1-800-CRIMESTOPPERS.

Flynn stared at Dale's picture on the front page. There she was, just as she had looked at the bar, lustrous hair sweeping down around her bare shoulders, knowing and sophisticated look intact, radiating that certain whatever-that-French-expression-was that still beat out younger actresses and had made one critic dub her "the thinking man's alternative to jail time," referring to the inundation of the media with practically pre-pubescent stars.

He put the paper down and his hand went reflexively to his cell phone. Should he call her number? But what would that do? Didn't other people have it too? Obviously they'd already tried every avenue to reach her. It was true she had told him he was getting her "private *private*" number, reserved only for those she "really *really* wanted to hear from," (as she had handed it over, he had been treated to that sizzling signature half-smile) and yet he hesitated. What if she *did* answer, or worse yet, some creepy male voice came on the line? He'd have to call the cops. That was the *last* thing he needed right now, to have his life get more complicated than it already was. He took a large gulp of his Starbucks. Better leave all that to the professionals.

The cappuccino was steaming and hot and full of white froth with a dusting of cinnamon, and ridiculously expensive, but the table bases were wrought iron and the tops were marble and there was a huge brass and copper samovar behind the counter, and Lorelei, Nicole's stoned and chain-smoking friend who always seemed to be taking a direct call from the Universe, had come over on her scooter (the one-footed kind) from Fort Greene.

Lorelei was the one friend of Nicole's who was impervious to her vitriolic critiques. She would listen attentively as Nicole explored the labyrinth of her life like Theseus minus the ball of thread. At this moment Nicole was revisiting what she considered to be the complete disaster of her open studio.

"It was a complete disaster. Of course it rained and ended up coming through the roof. So what else is new."

"But people came," insisted Lorelei.

"Yeah, like – *some* my friends. It was totally cool of you to come. But, like, a lot of other people …like fuckhead Ned didn't even stay to help clean up, Evan broke three wineglasses, just like last time, Harold and Holly had to get back to fucking New Haven, and Tom didn't come, he never goes to anything anymore. Then I had to watch Tara and David on the couch all night like they were the only two people in the world. Anyway, by the time the art dealers showed up, everything was ruined."

"What?!"

Nicole could tell by her friend's face that this bit of previously undisclosed information was the gold nugget of hope Lorelei was always certain could be found under the rampant turds of life.

"Art dealers came?? You didn't tell me that!"

"I know, but – "

"I *told* you sending out the postcards would work!!!!! You see!!! You just send out the positive energy and see what happens??!!!"

"Well, it rained. It ruined my paintings," repeated Nicole, refusing to give in. "Okay, a guy from some Manhattan gallery showed up and liked them but then it all went to shit. Literally. "

"Then he wasn't 'the one'," replied Lorelei, nodding sagely.

"The one *what?*" said Nicole, taking a sip of her cappuccino.

"The one who is supposed to help you." Lorelei reached for her pack of American Spirits. "I'm gonna go outside and have a cigarette. Wanna come?"

"It's okay, I'll hang here." She watched her friend, who had been single for a year, exit the café and ask for a light from a cute Greenpoint-type boy. Hope springs eternal, thought Nicole. Lorelei's unfailing positivity in the face of adversity never ceased to amaze her.

She had been holding off on telling Lorelei about Flynn. She had been periodically mentally retrieving his image like a hidden bar of chocolate, taking a bite now and then, holding off on cramming the whole thing in her mouth the way she wanted to.

To finish it and fully digest it would mean the processing and analyzing she had been avoiding – did he like her, was he gay, had she made a complete idiot out of herself - the whole gamut of questions that arose when she had an out-of-control crush.

Hoarding it to herself was like keeping her paintings hidden as she so often did, visible only to her eyes and the few friends that she trusted, away from the specter of harsh criticisms and non-understanding she always believed would follow any self-revelation.

But he *had* looked at her in an out-of-the-ordinary way, she thought, a direct, penetrating look she wasn't used to. He had cut through the barbed wire of her sarcasm, had made her follow him up to the roof, her velvet dress wet and dirty and dragging behind her.

He had offered to return to fix her skylight like helping someone out was a natural thing, an attitude practically non-existent in New York. It was something she had gotten a taste of for the first time when she moved to Brooklyn from Manhattan several years ago, along with neighbors who said hello, stoop sales with prices so low that they were really just a way of sharing what you had, and small eclectic shops with friendly and unconventional owners.

But these small town attributes were disappearing rapidly along with the less affluent classes, displaced and replaced with a new invasive species of yuppie. When Nicole had first migrated from Manhattan, and found that the first question out of everyone's mouths wasn't, "What do you do?" her joy had been unbounded. Being appreciated simply as a person was a new experience. But these days, without the proper trappings of cash, career, and condo, it seemed you were invisible.

Nicole suddenly wished she had a huge steaming mug of hot chocolate sitting in front of her instead of the coffee. All the fun of thinking about Flynn had gone, wrapped up in the web of her never-ending concerns. She was getting closer to the Minotaur of her own mind, she could feel it. Where was Lorelei when she needed her? She glanced out at the street and saw from Lorelei's stance and the angle of her cigarette as she talked to the boy that her friend would not be returning anytime soon.

Nicole stood up and reached for her bag. She had to get out of her head. She'd go down to the bridge over the Gowanus and paint. That was one good thing about being a part-time wage slave with no benefits. There was plenty of time to get lost in the few remaining unsanitized areas of New York.

Flynn didn't bother to respond when he walked in the Harmony doors and Kev and Seth declared that his bag looked like "piss and doody," plus was "faggy." The effort of pushing Dale and her fate out of his mind had lowered his threshold of tolerance for adolescent behavior.

He strode right to HH's door to ask for a meeting and when Harry barked out, "You got something? Finally!" and told him to close the door he seated himself in the second biggest chair in the office next to Harry's.

"There's…no one really looking after the place," he began. "The owner, Sally's out of town. She's in a place called Provincetown. My contact told me no one knows when she's coming back."

"Contact, huh?" said Harry, leaning back all the way in his chair, all of a sudden wishing desperately that he had a cigar in his mouth like he used to during private meetings. "Who're you talking to?"

"One of the girls that works there. She told me everything she knows. I guess there was just something about me that... invited confidence."

Harry grunted.

"They're planning a demonstration against the project. I don't know exactly when, but she said she'd keep me in the loop. It was great. She has no idea I work for you." Flynn crossed his ankle over his knee and also leaned back in his wide chair, but not quite as far as Harry.

"Good." Harry shook his head. "You know, kid, some people don't want to see opportunity when it's kicking them in the face. If someone came to me with an offer for a place as decrepit as that, hey... I'd take it, right? It's an eyesore, it's gotta be torn down anyway. But they always want more. What am I, Pippi Fucking Longstocking?! I don't have a suitcase full of gold coins sitting in my goddamn villa!"

"Well, she...Sally...kind of has a reason."

"Oh, yeah? What's that?"

"Well, because...it's a place...uh, that's kind of, irreplaceable. To her." Flynn struggled for the right words. "It's kind of like it's...important because it's..." how should he put this," 'different'." He grasped at Sally's words to Wendy. "It's like it's an 'underground thing.' "

Harry burst like a bull from his chair.

"You're fucking kidding me?! Christ! Now they're playing *that* card?"

"Card, sir?"

" 'Underground'!? What, now it's snaking through the city like a giant fucking white alligator?"

"Sir?"

"The goddamn 'underground railroad.' Oh, yeah," he railed. "Can't believe it, can you? That's the newest one! 'Can't touch it! Historic site!' They got a list, I'm telling you! You just wait," he wagged his finger at Flynn. "They find out that isn't true, next thing: 'Oh, the Pilgrims had a pet cemetery here!' Bull's balls!" He came rocketing out from behind his desk and began stalking up and down in front of Flynn. Flynn sat up and hurriedly put his leg down to make room for Harry's trajectory.

"This is it, though!" his boss exclaimed. "Enough! If they won't go, I'll make 'em go. You," he pointed at Flynn, "will keep doing what you're doing. Keep watch. Keep getting them to talk to you. And I – " he raised his finger to the ceiling, " 'as God is my witness, as God is my witness they're not going to lick me. I'm going to live through this and when it's all over, I'll never be hungry again.' " His huge stomach quivered as he walked. " 'No, nor any of my folk. If I have to lie, steal, cheat or kill. As God is my witness, I'll never be hungry again!' "

Sir John, Sophia, and Humphrey had all been wrenched from their slumber, and their pitiful eyes following his every move infuriated Harry even more.

"*This* bull," he cried, pointing at his chest, "is not dozing! LET THE BULLDOZING BEGIN!"

Buzz hated Mondays. But that was okay because he also hated Tuesdays, Wednesdays, Thursdays and Fridays. In fact any day that he had to act out the charade of his so-called "job," the nepotistic toy that had been forced on him in a failed attempt to make him into someone he wasn't raised to be: responsible, hard-working, and happy to be in close proximity to his dad.

His excuses for not being at work had been wearing thinner than truffle shavings on a hundred dollar burger. It was increasingly difficult for his father to believe Buzz's reports of how he spent his days when he was consistently vague and had hardly anything to show for it. The only thing that had kept him afloat over the months was his success in selling condos to some of his gay friends, and also his relentless skill at talking up investment opportunities to people who hadn't previously owned a building, but quickly learned the advantages of being on the right side of the property price/mortgage ratio. It was an extra perk that once invested, their previous fury was replaced with joy at the sight of the obscene sums required to live in their neighborhoods. It was a case of the "if you can't beat 'em, join 'em," mentality, and New York City had become more and more a place where beating the inequities was impossible and altering one's outlook was the simplest alternative to leaving.

Luckily for Buzz, no change in his values was required. He had learned from birth that money was the most important thing on earth. Like many rich families, there was no delight taken in their ready access to various funds and trusts, rather, an unshakeable belief that there was

"Let the bulldozing begin!"

never enough, along with a sense of entitlement laced with the constant fear that what they had would somehow go away. On top of that, like pre-grated Parmesan cheese found in the refrigerated aisle of the supermarket, the suspicion that all people they knew wanted to use them covered everything with a taste slightly reminiscent of vomit.

His homosexuality had really been the one thing that had saved him up to this point; it was different, no one talked about it, and he felt a satisfaction at being able to live a life in which his father did not play the slightest part. His sister had been allowed to cutely flaunt her lesbianism, their father accepted it with a shrug as many men who considered themselves Conservative had done for decades, especially since it was not uncommon for their wives to have had leanings of their own in the past. Rich girls did pretty much anything they wanted. Their partying and parade of inappropriate lovers before settling down was practically a tradition. But Buzz's father had no interest at all in his son's emotional life, if in fact he knew that he had one; Harry was distanced enough that he had never given his son's sexuality the slightest thought. They had nothing in common except money, and since it was a given that their lives would revolve around it, no in-depth conversation between them need ever take place.

Out of the crucible of his emptiness, Buzz had emerged with a kind of determination to forge his own identity from the outside in, to create an image of himself with material things that would come together like pieces of a puzzle to show him what he was. This new apartment he was stalking online would be a major piece of his yet unfinished personality.

Despite the fact that he didn't yet have the chunk of cash he would need to complete the purchase, he decided today to keep the feel-good going by beginning the acquisition of the requisite accessories, the first, and most obvious of these, being a purebred little dog. It had become a required accoutrement, like a handbag or a wallet, people looked strange without one when out walking. Added to that was the fact that Manhattan was such a police state now that loitering of any sort, even innocent cruising, was looked upon with suspicion. The exception was that an idling, wealthy-looking person could still saunter about pulling at the throat of a trailing, ignored animal, while discussing plans or meetings on this week's gadget, with invisible and highly important business associates. Lastly, and perhaps most gratifyingly, a dog would replace sexual submissives as his new semi-distraction from what he always felt was the cesspool of himself.

Buzz stood before the window of Tiny Lovers on the far East end of Christopher Street, an upscale boutique for aspiring city dog-owners whose under-sized apartments and lack of imagination had dotted the landscape of Manhattan with look-alike pets.

A baby pug tilted its head and looked up at him from its nest of paper curls. Despite its lack of high cheekbones, Buzz found the need in its expression not quite an instant turn-off as he did with homo sapiens, homo or otherwise.

As he contemplated this departure from his usual reaction, he felt something odd: a soft touch on his knee that caused him to turn sharply. A wide, wet nose was sniffing him below the belt, and it wasn't Tonio's. It was a big, black, limping mutt with of all god-awful things, a rainbow scarf tied around its neck. Buzz's eye traveled up the leash to meet a shy and apologetic grin.

"Oh, God, Harvey! Stop it. STOP! He is just *horrible!*" said Harvey's owner, meaning, like all dog owners, the exact opposite.

Harvey nuzzled against Buzz's thigh.

"Don't worry, he's friendly!"

"Apparently," said Buzz.

"Ooh, she's cute!" said the man, looking at the pup in the window, who was still gazing at Buzz.

"It's a she?" said Buzz, with distaste.

"Isn't she gorgeous? Girl dogs are great. I don't know why, but for some reason, with the girls, it's not all about *them* every second."

"Mm-hm." Buzz wouldn't have been caught dead talking to this man. If only he had seen him coming.

"Harvey is an exception, though. Most mutts are. They just bond with you, you know? If you are looking for unconditional love, and who isn't, a rescue dog is the way to go."

Unconditional love? Rescue dog? thought Buzz to himself. "I'm looking for a particular breed," he replied stiffly.

"Oh, which one?"

Buzz had no idea.

"Actually, you can get all kinds of breeds, even purebreds, as rescues now. It's so sad, people get them and then they don't want to take care of them. It's so heartbreaking. Dogs are companions. They love you and then they expect to be with you for life, don't you, Harvey?" The man rubbed the top of his mutt's head. "I thought it would be so cute to get a little white dog, also, and call him 'Milk,' but Harvey needs a lot of love and I don't want him to be jealous."

Buzz was more than ready to beat his retreat from this surfeit of sharing.

"If you want," the man continued, "I can hook you up with this guy who has purebred rescues. We have to stop the cycle of puppy mills…"

Buzz was in the process of rolling his eyes upwards and turning towards Sixth Avenue when he heard the man saying:

"…plus you only have to pay an adoption fee of like a hundred dollars. These are like two or three thousand."

The ins and outs of the emotional life of dogs had not moved Buzz in the slightest. But here was something he could relate to. After all, the only thing worse than talking about money was not talking about it when the situation demanded it.

"I'm Rick, by the way," said the man, holding out his hand.

The god-awful rainbow kerchief and now the god-awful name. But the prospect of spending money was even more awful for a rich man who deserved everything gratis.

Buzz's cold and limp handshake met Rick's warm one.

"He actually lives right here…right around the corner."

Buzz looked up and saw the street sign. He made no attempt to hide his grimace. "Gay Street." Of course. It would be.

It was a simple walk from Nicole's studio to the Gowanus. She followed the street straight down to a bridge over the waterway. It had begun to cloud up, but that was how Nicole liked it. It brought out the colors in a deeper, richer way.

It was a good idea to keep coming down here now too because it was only a matter of time before it changed completely. The word was that it had been eyed as "the next Venice," but by who? That was always the question. Venice, Las Vegas-style? Most likely. Little chance that there'd be delicate and exquisite palaces mirrored in this water.

As she set up her easel, she was conscious of the low-grade anxiety that was becoming a standard for artists in New York City. She hated it that the climate was now such that she felt nervous when setting up in a public place. At any moment she might be startled by the sudden materialization of a police vehicle and a stentorian command to remove the "unauthorized" object, or be harassed for a license or permit of some sort. Really?? Is this view, too, owned, she thought, as she arranged her palette and squeezed out an extra-thick line of Prussian Blue. By standing here was she violating a new statute? Obstructing the view from a brand-new co-op? Flaunting some sort of defiance she wasn't even aware of?

Or perhaps she was a terrorist recruit secretly recording the geometry of a waterway suspiciously close to the target of Manhattan. Any moment now there should be helicopters overhead, scanning her irises from a range of hundreds of feet, instantly transmitting information to a vast data bank:

Nicole DeGioia. Clickclackclack. Female. 27 years of age BEEP. Height: 5 feet and 4.32566600 inches. Hair: Dark Brown. Eyes: Blue. Felonies: None. Click clack. Did in fact steal a cheap rhinestone necklace from the drugstore once when she was twelve. Beep. Claimed in therapy theft was due to father's neglect BEEP. Therapist encouraged this view BEEP. Therapist had previously been recorded on surveillance video accepting newspaper advocating Socialism at anti-war rally BEEP BEEP BEEP BEEP…

Tom, her artist friend who had not attended her open house because he rarely left his apartment anymore, was an "alternative violinist," who had been told by police in the West 4th Street subway station in Manhattan that he must cease his playing because the vibrations from his stringed instrument would cause structural damage to the station. "SERIOUSLY???" Nicole recalled saying to him as he lay curled up in a ball on the rough Astroturf –like black carpet of his closet-like studio in the East Village, where pale diamonds of white light were refused entry by the steel accordion window gate like Bridge and Tunnelers pressing to get in a pretentious, "exclusive" club.

They are pushing us underground. Soon we will be like the mole people, the mole artists, and our studios and workplaces and homes will be layered levels deep in the earth where we will crawl down to complete the visions that for some reason still exalt life.

A gaggle of bicyclists speeding across the bridge roused her from her ruminations and she blinked. She squeezed smudges of Volcano Red and Earth Brown onto her palette. For her, the beauty of these abandoned and neglected landscapes was largely due to the combination of the absence of humans and the layers of history gently sanded down by time.

The colors themselves were reason enough for a painter to come down here; uncut by high rises, the sky was spread out overhead, as if reminding viewers that nature could not be stopped at the gates of urbanity. The unobstructed light reached down and touched each structure in a different and unique way: the rich brick red and brown of the old warehouses; the black weather-beaten water towers with their huge, round, squat, oddly comforting shapes, sitting atop buildings like mothers watching over their children below; the commercial signs of other eras whose tints were still appealing; the concrete white of one and two story buildings casting their long, low shadows on the pavement in front of them in the afternoons.

To Nicole, the entire area around the canal appeared like the archaeological dig of a lost civilization. She found it just as entrancing as if she were viewing a newly discovered tomb of American history, with its relics of thriving manufacturing intertwined with the life of a once vital waterway. She certainly wasn't among the first to appreciate this area. Painters had been coming here for years, bringing their new eye to the world of the past.

She was filling in the outlines of two abandoned silos when she heard the harsh drone of a helicopter approaching. It carried with it the intensity of a wasp on a spring day.

SERIOUSLY???

But it passed over where she stood and she watched as it briefly hovered over points further West and then circled back around and flew South low over the canal until it disappeared. That was no lazy tourist sight seer, that was for damn sure.

She sighed. Fuck. New York these days was so exhausting. Everyone was on a fucking mission.

True to his pronouncement, Harry began to move into position minutes after Flynn, a bit discomfited at the real-life effect his espionage work had set in motion, and irrationally aggravated that he had not been instantaneously promoted, had left the office.

"Let your fingers do the walking." Harry remembered this old chestnut from Ma Bell as he thumbed through his worn address book looking for a particular name among the many that were listed in no particular order. The Bell Telephone Yellow Pages slogan was an echo of another time, the days before goddamn computers, when all you needed was paper and a desk and a phone on it, and he had refused to change his old working habits, even the name of his company, against the advice of many. The good old days when businesses still had family names. Johnson and Johnson. Ford. Bloomingdale's. Before the names of companies were indistinguishable from those of anti-psychotic drugs. Come to think of it, Verizon sounded just like something that would flat line a crazy person in milliseconds. It even rhymed with the equally flat "horizon." Esso, the gently-named gas company he remembered fondly from his childhood, with its little winged horse, had become "EXXON" – which could, perhaps, be a drug used for lethal injection in capital punishment cases. Exonerate, ex-con…maybe not. But end-of-the-alphabet letters were very popular. There was something final about them. Valium: the perfect name for a gated community.

It had been suggested at one point by a marketing exec he had hired to promote a particularly pricey new condo cluster that he change Harmony to something more noticeable and bold, and at the same time corporate-sounding and anonymous, something that could be successfully identified as a "brand." Never. "Who needs the fucking marketing flaks," Harry spoke out loud, as he finally found the name he was looking for in his address book.

He knew what he had to do. He'd realize the vision that the architects had laid down before him in a model just like the Lego set he'd enjoyed as a boy, clean and orderly, square and hermetically sealed and yet dotted with humanizing details like miniature trees and tiny tony cars in the soon-to-be mammoth parking lot. Even smaller than the trees and cars were the miniscule people, some even with infinitesimal pooches that dotted the periphery of the perfect, white, model. The store names fronted the street and had exact logo replicas. Numerous chains had already bought in and would be waiting like virgin brides on a wedding night, their pristine aisles wide and inviting, welcoming their yuppie grooms.

The pages of his book were crammed full with blue inky half-smudged names. Attorneys, architects, financial advisers, insurance executives, city agency heads, judges, etc, etc, etc. The human components of getting business done. When you got right down to it though, most of these people were bottom feeders. No, for this he'd have to go directly to the Orcas whose gaping mouths he had filled with enough bread and fishes, so to speak, to piss off Jesus. To make sure the way was clear, you get the go-ahead from the biggies. They made sure you didn't get caught in any nets. Films, buildings, what the hell was the difference? Once you got *them* in your corner the lower levels were like pulling levers on rigged slot machines. The gold just came pouring out into your hands.

It was at the moment he'd reached for the phone that there was a knock on his door, and Helen Haliburton entered the room unannounced. Mrs. Haliburton was a fearlessly independent woman, especially since the death of her husband. Unsatisfied with the properties she had been shown by Flynn, she had determined that she would seek out the most powerful man in the company, and get what she wanted that way, as she had done so many times before. When the interests of the individual were ignored she would not back down; she considered it Un-American.

"Mr. Harmony. Helen Haliburton." She held out her gloved hand in a regal manner and as if pulled by a magnet, Harry rose to his feet. "It is *such* a pleasure to meet you," she continued, leaning slightly over his desk until a whiff of expensive perfume floated under his nose. She touched him lightly on the arm. "I *know* I've come to the right person." She looked up through her mascara-ed lashes to fix his eyes with a soft yet penetrating gaze. At the same time she allowed a small, tight smile to come to her lips.

Like most property owners, Harry as a rule reacted badly to any hint of need. Their days were filled with a million and one duties, and they more often than not felt put-upon and victimized both by the rules and regulations of the city and even more so by the endless task of managing what they owned. Despite their often extreme wealth, it never quite seemed to compensate them fully for their trouble.

And yet now, enveloped in a cloud of fragrance and taking in the gold and undoubtedly real precious stones of the abundant jewelry that adorned her and her immaculate ladies' suit under her gauzy but wide-brimmed hat, his ingrained irritation was unable to rise to the surface. She was wealthy, that might make her important, and, as evidenced by her stare, she was looking into his soul. There would be no hiding from *this* woman. Simultaneously with this thought came the fearful consideration that she could be a reporter.

"As my late husband Carl Haliburton the Fifth used to say," she continued, "there are three kinds of men – men who find gold, men who find oil, and men who find the men who find oil and gold. May I take a seat?"

"Please," barked out Harry. Haliburton? Wasn't that the name associated with obscene amounts of both money and scandal, with a massive dose of government connection thrown in? He'd better be careful. "Bogart!" he yelled at his slumbering dog, who was collapsed on the largest of the leather armchairs, and opened one weary and partially bloodshot eye, only to close it again.

"Ah wouldn't dream of it, Mr. Harmony," said Mrs. Haliburton, waving a hand in dismissal of his order. "The poor thing looks so tired and old. I'll just perch myself right here." The chair was the one closest to Harry, in fact, one on which he often placed his feet, but she briskly brushed any dirt from its surface. "I have got such a soft spot for mature dogs," she said, seating herself lightly on its edge. "So much more appreciative than young puppies. All they need is a little rub under the chin and they are just as happy as can be." To illustrate, her smooth and polished nails coated with "Lilac Blush" found Bogart's jowls and scratched among the triple folds of white fur. His tongue lolled outwards and he gave an almost embarrassing whine of pleasure. "Well, Mr. Harmony, you strike me as the type of man who could find oil all on his own."

"I do all right," said Harry. With difficulty, he wrenched his eyes away from hers. "How can I help you?"

"I am looking for an oasis in the desert. A home for my child. And after what your man Mr. Sharpe showed me this past week, I've almost despaired of ever finding that special spot."

"Sharpe, huh?" Harry wondered who she was talking about.

"That's the one! *Absolutely* charming, but I have a feeling there are some properties reserved for, how shall I put this, the best of the best."

"Uh-*huh*." Was this some sort of racial code? Were they staking him out for entrapment? He wouldn't put it past those bastards. If so, they were barking up the wrong tree. If there was one thing he didn't have a tolerance for, besides liberals, it was discrimination of any kind. Most particularly, the kind which got in the way of business. Money was one color, green.

"Do you have a child, Mr. Hahmony?"

Harry gave an odd sort of snort. "Two. My daughter, Wilhemina. She's a good kid. Likes to do what she likes to do, you know? But so what? Then there's the other one."

"Well," continued Helen, "I don't know what yours have been up to but my Ivy is finally done with what they call an education these days, which really means she's learned one-hundred and one ways to spend her parents' money. And now that she's leaving Atlanta, which they call a cosmopolitan city because it no longer has any character, she wants to come up North. I can't imagine why. Good Lord, there's not even a Neiman Marcus. No offense meant, or course."

She was much too loquacious to be a reporter, thought Harry. He knew all too well how that sector worked. They got you to open your mouth too wide and watched while you screwed yourself with your own tongue like the voyeuristic word whores they were. So now what?

In spite of himself he found he was attracted to Mrs. Haliburton. She seemed soft, like a big downy pillow, and she was wearing colors, unlike 99 percent of the women in New York with their relentless black. Had anyone ever asked a man what he thought of black? Anyway, it was a relief to watch her, almost restful, and her jewelry dangled and shook gently when she talked creating a soporific effect, like a mobile above a baby's crib. He should try to be more conversational.

"So where's she living now?"

"In some God-awful shack she shares with three sisters from her sorority in what they imagine is the 'bohemian' part of town, which really means they pay luxury rent to climb five flights and go without heat."

"Three roommates, huh?" grunted Harry. "She must be climbing the walls."

His little joke was rewarded by a peal of appreciative laughter from Mrs. Haliburton. "Ivy – climbing the walls – now isn't that clever? I must say it's been a long time since I've met a man with a sense of humor. Poor Carl, God rest his soul, never did know how to take things lightly. What finally felled him was when one of the Skull and Bones men called him up to tell him his stocks had lost fifty percent of their value. I'll never forget that day. It was April 1st... those boys could be so cruel."

"I'm sorry for your loss." Harry felt his stomach grumble. In the usual scheme of things this would be the signal for him to close his door and ferret into the depths of the mini-refrigerator he kept stashed away in the small room behind him. And yet... it would be rude, came the unexpected thought, and Harry's mind had a moment of paralysis as this rare consideration presented itself.

"Mrs. Haliburton – " Harry paused, but no invitation to "call me Helen" came, "may I take you to lunch?"

"Well..."

Harry stood up and gallantly motioned towards the door.

"Don't put any calls through!" Harry shouted to a surprised staff, as they passed through the office, especially since there was no secretary or receptionist. He remembered at the nick of time to hold open the door and let her pass through first.

"A Northern gentleman! What a find!" To his shock, Helen slipped her arm through his. It had been a long time since he had been touched that way by a woman. It made him feel both sad and excited. Ironically, for someone who had lived in Hollywood for so long, he had become sick to death of happy endings.

Flynn spent the rest of the day hosting a series of open houses for those anxious to become part of the growing community of home-owning Slopers. While various would-be buyers darted competitively through each property, he contemplated going to visit his father. He'd only been home once since his move back to Brooklyn. He was feeling guilty, but his dislike for his stepmother had so far wrestled that guilt to the ground and done a victory dance each time he was about to go.

He couldn't stand to see the way his father let himself be treated: the constant berating and put-downs, her selfish, hard voice insisting that nothing was ever done right. Add to that the fact that she felt entitled to comment in each and every way on everyone else's life: she had already harped on Flynn's fall from financial grace at the same time letting it be known that she approved of real estate as a career without including Flynn himself in her approbation. "Oh, real estate," she had crowed. "That's a very good business, if you know what you're doing."

His father's passivity in the face of her abuse never ceased to anger and amaze him, and he had broached the subject several times in the years since that unhappy day of marriage, but his Dad shrugged it off. "She means well," he'd say.

She was so different from his Mom, thought Flynn, as he pressed number four on his speed dial while trying to avoid being knocked over by the hungry consumers ranting breathlessly on their cell phones to significant others or brokers. She couldn't have been more different if you sat down and made a list:

1. His Mom: overly generous; prone to giving away anything and everything and could never say no vs. his step-mother: selfish and entitled, saying the word no was akin to orgasm, thus saying it over and over again was finally explained.

2. Mom: Super sensitive to the point of major mood swings; happiness became laughter and smiles and flowers around the house, anger became days of depression and sadness vs. his step-mother's demented war-like demeanor, always ready to drain the blood out of some hapless peasant who had unknowingly strayed onto the Vlad-the-Impaler estate of her personality.

3. His mother's growing dependence on alcohol and pills to smooth over the hurts of life vs. being the person who relished inflicting pain.

Flynn had always vowed never to get involved with a woman like that. It was true that his first choice of mate had proved unfortunate, but Constance had been more of an ice queen than anything else. He could have stayed in her frozen castle; it wouldn't have been too painful, he would only have grown numb.

"Hey, Dad," said Flynn. He watched as two white blond women with double strollers and husbands in tow pushed their way through the apartment with all the care and subtlety of German tanks rolling into soon-to-be occupied territory. Unfortunately they both reached the door to the second bedroom at exactly the same moment. Both refused to move. The usual instantaneous bond between such couples forged by similarities in race, income, and baby-making frenzy would not, could not, survive this moment.

"I was thinking of coming around Wednesday night," he said, keeping an eye peeled for an incipient melee. "Is Susan going to be there?"

"She's always here," said his Dad. "When isn't she here?"

"I don't know… I just thought…"

"It's four years already, when're you gonna learn to like her? What time are you coming over?"

"I don't know." Flynn's will was fading at the reality of facing the Gorgon's head.

"Oh, by the way, I found some things of your mother's."

The standoff between the two women now reached a climax. They faced each other with mirroring frowns, stroller wheels locked. The husbands ventured cautiously into the fray, sticking the toes of would-be brotherly camaraderie gingerly into the piranha-infested waters.

"We'll just wait out here," said one.

"Thanks, man."

"Logan has to get to day camp," hissed one of the men's wife.

"Parker's nanny is coming at four," countered the other.

"Dad, I'll call you back," said Flynn.

Saved by the hell. The subject of his mother's things still in the house suddenly put into perspective just how unimportant, if repellent, all this privileged jockeying for position was.

"We have another open house in the building, ladies, starting in a few minutes," he said. "Ground floor. That one has *three* bedrooms and a backyard."

"Why didn't you tell us about that before?!"

"I can't believe it!"

The mothers looked at each other in amazement, bonded by their shock and disbelief. Peace had been restored to the valley, at least until they got downstairs.

As the thumping and rattling of their descent subsided, Flynn was left to stand by himself on the hastily refinished floor, the white glare from the sun slanting in through the bare windows. The market was so hot there was no need to fix it up for a showing – it'd fly out of here regardless. He was glad they'd left, even more so when his cell rang and he saw that it was Wendy calling him. His cover needed to be maintained now more than ever; the last thing he needed was some desperate yuppie yelling questions about common charges at him loud enough to be heard over the line.

"Hey… Wendy! Good to hear from you. How're things?"

"Yo, Flynn, how you doing? You get home okay the other night? Oh, shit! You was pretty wasted! Listen, I'm calling everyone personal. That meeting I told you about? You know, for the protest for the building? It's gonna be Wednesday."

"Oh, really… Great!"

"Man, I hope a lotta people come."

"Definitely. Can't have enough people at a protest!"

"Right? Okay, so like, seven o'clock. Yeah, you know," said Wendy. "We gotta do this for the community."

"Sure. Hey - is Sally going to be there by any chance?"

"I don't know. I gotta ask Pat. Thas her partner. Yo, I see you there. Yo, tell your friends to come. That way people gonna know the bullshit is going on."

"Sure, I will."

"Alright. Later. See you. Power to the people. Thas what Sally always say."

As he walked out onto the street, Flynn gathered his thoughts about the protest. He had to go, of course, but could he ask a lot of questions without making these people suspicious? Did these types even think that way? Or was everyone they didn't know their friend, the way he was now Wendy's? If Sally didn't make it that could be a good sign. It might be an indication that she was tired of fighting. She'd have to give up and take an offer eventually. If not…he might find out some damaging information. Unpaid taxes, violations of safety codes, fire hazards, etc. In New York, landlords were always being cited for something. There was always drama in the papers: tenants being evicted, conducting rent strikes, or getting burned out of their houses…that last, of course, was always a *bad* story…

He could hear the yelps and cries of the parents and children downstairs. A female broker from the company was showing the place. Flynn didn't envy her. He might or might make a sale today, but it really didn't matter. He was making progress on the assignment that would make or break him. He had no one to call to tell about it, though. No one to celebrate with. Kev or Seth would have made straight for a stripper bar.

He went straight home. As he put his key in the lock of the apartment he was surprised to hear rock music playing loudly inside. He stepped back and checked the number on the door. Had he got off on the wrong floor? He had never heard Barnaby play music in the house, he knew nothing about his musical tastes except for the off-putting t-shirts he wore displaying the names and logos of animal rights bands that were so graphic Flynn could hardly bring himself to look at them.

Was there a party going on? Should he just go back out? He feared a contingent of similarly-minded young people, all sitting wearing black, staring at him and his leather shoes. And he'd planned to microwave a burger! What now? He pressed his ear to the door and strained to hear the lyrics. "I shot off a piece of that dead cow's eye…" Good God!

Whatever. He decided he was too exhausted to care.

But when he turned the key and pushed the door open there was no one in sight, the sound was coming solely from Barnaby's bedroom, and in fact it was Led Zeppelin singing I sure'd like a piece of your custard pie, not Garroted Goat or Jesus Bacon at all. Well, that was a relief. But wasn't custard made with eggs?

No matter. He stretched out on the sofa and closed his eyes, imagining that he heard, as he nodded off, the sound of a female voice mixed in with the music. He must be dreaming. But there it was again, an unmistakably female giggle. Christ. Even the vegan celibate was getting laid.

CHAPTER FIVE

It was all new to Flynn: raw cauliflower, hummus soaking through paper plates. A dish based on eggplant that everyone ignored. The chaotic pre-meeting milling about; the mix of intensely happy socializing coupled with the sharing of dark news involving deaths and beatings of gays worldwide; discussions about the most recent lost or won court cases; the endless wait for late arrivals in an effort to include everyone's "voice," and rules for speaking, gone over slowly, very slowly, agonizingly slowly, all of which left very little time to plan the protest.

But as Flynn watched, silent in his corner, it all somehow came together. One person offered to make the flyers, others said they'd wheat paste around the area, an email tree for spreading the word was organized, and people were reminded to make signs and banners to bring on the day. It was a community stone soup, begun with a basic stock of outrage and thickened with the pureed vegetables of frustration. It was much, much milder than Flynn had expected. Where were the eye-catching radicals he always saw on the news, shoving tofu in police officers' faces while wearing red communist-looking kerchiefs to hide from the FBI?

It seemed so smooth and harmonious. But when the actual date and time was about to be voted on, there was suddenly a disruption from a vocal member of the group who had already managed to hog a chunk of time, with various concerns that were all very minor and somewhat distracting.

"I want to talk about the trans fats issue!!"

"What?" said the gay woman who had been elected after some discussion to be the facilitator for the second half of the meeting.

"How they're saying trans fats are banned everywhere!!"

A blank look travelled over the faces of the protestors.

Flynn couldn't help himself. "What does that have to do with –" he began.

"Don't try to silence me!!!" the woman thundered. "Trans fats is a feminist and civil rights issue!!"

"Is it – is it," said one very young girl with a nose ring and pink hair with an admirable and yet doomed attempt to understand, "is it because you feel we should be able to eat whatever we want? Because choice is important."

"You can't ban us!!!!" said the woman, rising to her feet. "If you're not comfortable with the trans community, whatever weight we choose to be, you are just as guilty as the media and the straight world and everyone else who is trying to deny us our rights!!!"

It took a minute before the misinterpretation was decoded.

"Trans fats isn't about people," began one gay man.

"How dare you! How can you dehumanize us like that!"

"No, it's about food, they're trying to get restaurants to not put -"

At this point the group devolved into a volley of explanations.

"Quiet!!!!!!!!!!!!!!!!" yelled the facilitator. "Deborah, we respect your issues. However, our agenda which we voted on earlier, lists choosing the date and time of the protest as an order of business that has not yet been voted on. So I propose we postpone the discussion of this issue until we can vote on discussing it. Those in favor, please raise your hands. Discussion postponed. Those who would like to discuss when we will discuss discussing the issue, please write your name and number down on the piece of paper we will pass around. Next item for discussion. We need to take a vote now so we can make sure we're organized and ready. All those in favor of voting on voting now - "

At that moment all the lights in Aunt Muffin's suddenly went dark.

"Shit," said Wendy, emerging from the bathroom, zipping up her fly. "Wha' happen to the fucking lights, man? I think I whizzed on some guy standin' next to me."

In the ensuing chaos the facilitator yelled for a vote to table the vote. Flynn pushed through the crowd. What the hell had happened? People were bubbling over with discussion about the sudden plunge into darkness, but Flynn had to make his way out alone, keeping the low profile he'd assumed to avoid detection. He felt a sudden tinge of melancholy as he turned up a quiet side street. It was good, though, for him to take an alternate route: that way he'd be able to avoid seeing anyone from the meeting.

Except for one.

It was Deborah, the living, breathing embodiment of everything that was wrong with radical politics, taking off the baseball cap with the rainbow pin, the thick pink-rimmed glasses and bright purple shirt she had been wearing, stuffing them into a bag, and getting into the back seat of a Lincoln Town car with dark windows that stopped in front of her.

Buzz was waiting in the back seat.

"How did it go?" he said.

"Good enough."

The car pulled into traffic.

"I told you!" Buzz sniggered. "'Trans fats.' I'm a fucking genius!"

"Don't get a big head about it."

"I've got more where that came from."

After a couple of blocks the car pulled to a stop and "Deborah" handed Buzz an envelope. Buzz looked inside and counted the money greedily.

"So, what's our next move?" he said, stuffing it into the pocket inside his jacket.

"We'll let you know," she answered.

"Don't forget, I'm your man," said Buzz as he slid out. "I've got total access, I can get whatever information from the Harmony files that you want."

"We'll let you know," said the driver with a voice that was like a cold whisper on velvet, and drove off into the approaching night.

Nicole hadn't been able to finish the painting she'd started on the bridge, so tonight she'd sworn she'd get the rest of it done, just as a fuck you to the helicopter that had circled back around three and four times more until it had begun to drive her crazy and she'd had to leave. She'd been too stressed out from the noise and annoyance to speculate further about Homeland Security's rapidly growing files on young white artsy liberals; she'd just grabbed her easel and paints, and retreated.

Finishing it hadn't been easy. She'd been painting furiously in the uncomfortably warm room, and then stumbled back down to her apartment where she made straight for her bed.

The phone on her fire escape began ringing just as she'd started her confused dreams of helicopters and lurking "security" men. It had been happening a lot recently, the calls, especially very late at night and into the wee hours of the morning. They'd all been hang-ups, and it was beginning to freak her out. She didn't get up to answer it.

Sometime later another call came. The sound was relentless, and as often happens in sleep she thought she had arisen, torturously, and was actually getting up and going to the phone and picking it up and yelling STOP FUCKING CALLING ME.

But finally it was too real to ignore, and despite her exhaustion she fought to come awake, and at first she felt newly victimized but it was a pain that she had to deal with as no one else was there, as usual, and so anger came to her rescue, as it always did. Eyes still half-closed, she pushed off her covers and strode to the window. She would pick up the phone and not say anything, just listen, to see who blinked first. She grabbed the bottom of the decrepit window frame and jerked it upwards and nearly sprained her wrists. It was completely sealed shut.

The closest pay phone was two and a half blocks away. She'd never had a cell phone; that was just another bullshit way to isolate you.

Ned answered with the strange cautious tone of voice people reserve for when they make the brave choice to take a call from an unrecognized number.

"Hello?" he said, as if he was an old lady opening her door and peering out from behind its chain lock.

"Fuck Ned, why'd you take so long to pick up?"

"Nicky? You're lucky I picked up at all. I didn't recognize the number. Where are you calling from?"

"The fucking street. Listen, I think someone did something to my window."

"What?"

"Like, nailed it shut or something. And yesterday, I was painting and all of a sudden all the lights went out."

"Are you having your period?"

"Fuck you. The fucking phone was ringing again. Remember the calls?"

"I kind of don't remember."

"I told you. I keep getting all these hang-up calls. Shit, Ned, I'm scared. Can you come over?"

"I'd love to, babe, but the Weeves are coming over for a power breakfast in a couple hours."

106

"Seriously ? And that's more important than me being in danger? I can't fucking believe you."

"Wait – babe, don't hang up. I'm sorry. The window? Which one?"

"The one onto the fucking fire escape." Nicole felt tears begin to threaten. "I tried to open it because the phone woke me up and I was like, I'm going to find out who this is or do something and then it wouldn't open."

"Sounds like it was just stuck, babe. Did you take a look at it?"

"How can I look at it when I can't get out there because it won't open?" Nicole swallowed hard and wiped away a tear with the wide sleeve of the vintage kimono she'd thrown on over her jeans.

"Wow, babe. I wish I could come over, I really do, but it sounds like you're just really stressed out. Don't get mad…but… you…sound a little paranoid."

Nicole's head swam. Was he right? She sniffed. "I'm going to call Lorelei."

"Good idea. Why don't you go out for a latte? If I was still in Billyburg I'd just hop on the Vespa, you know? The East Village is just so much further away."

"Actually, it's not, Ned." She was regaining her strength, if only the kind necessary to participate in a mundane couples' argument. "And it's *not* the East Village. It's the Lower East Side. Don't you know that was all about bullshit real estate?"

"Nicky, it's not even noon. Can you give it a rest?"

"Oh, but it's okay when you start ranting about how the Weevils are so misunderstood by the mainstream at eight in the morning…"

"I've got a call coming in. I gotta go."

Lorelei's approach to Nicole's troubles couldn't have been more different than Ned's. Ned skated over the concrete details of his life like he was taking an amateur turn on the ice; it was only when he cast his line into the fishing hole of the music world that he became interested in what lay under the surface. And yet, his astounding ability to project his own ideas and opinions onto bands, in a way combined his mental DNA with theirs, to create a sort of mutant baby for which he showed all the care and pride of a new parent. As the baby grew, he exhibited the typical alternative rock critic's joy in exercising his creativity and making a mountain out of a molehill, by applying four or six years' worth of wasted higher education onto whoever was updating yeah yeah yeah that month. As far as his own experiences went, his rent, his clothes, his attitude towards his life and his girlfriends, had all been settled on years ago, and saw no hope of changing. In short, for him, as for millions of adults and adolescents and adult-adolescents in America, the semi-real world of images had been deemed more worthy of attention than his own.

Lorelei, by contrast, kept an eye on other kinds of stars, the ones in the sky. Her observations were translated into a mix of predictions, psychology, and counseling, but all for a practical purpose. Today, she listened to Nicole's torment-of-the-hour and stared at the cinnamon pattern on her cappuccino as if she could decode answers in even that microcosmic spiral.

"There you go!" she threw up her hands in emphasis as Nicole slowed her story to a halt. "Aries is in your third house! There could be all kinds of things coming to 'attack' you over the next few weeks. But, you have a lot of Libra too! Try using that to make more connections, and, use the ones you already have for extra strength."

"I already get free coffee at work. Ha-ha."

Lorelei peered at her intensely. "You can always stay at my place, you know."

Nicole smiled. "I know. Thanks, honey. You're so cool, as always." Lorelei lived in a rambling floor-through up six flights of stairs, with a plethora of revolving roommates and dream-catchers in every corner. The downstairs doors were never locked, and occasional shots rang out in the vicinity.

Nicole wouldn't take her up on the offer, of course. Her nerves were already on edge. But the flush of good feeling from being cared about almost prompted her to tell her friend that Flynn was coming over that night. Almost. But then, it would just be worse when the inevitable disappointment the "universe" had in store for her arrived.

Harry summoned both Flynn and Buzz into his office late that afternoon. Buzz made his entrance replete with his newest purchase: a hyper-active miniature pinscher that growled and darted maniacally at each human being within reach of its pointy, vicious-looking teeth. Harry's three sedentary bulldogs also received a blast of likely obscene doggie-speak and slunk instantly under Harry's desk and closer to his wide, trousered legs.

Buzz's quest for a cut-rate canine had not gone well. After a brief interview with the old-timey gay who rescued dogs and lived in a basement apartment that had last seen redecoration in 1973, he had been rejected out of hand by the man who had informed Rick that he was looking for actual human beings who cared about animals to be parents to his saved pooches.

"When I asked him why he wanted a dog he looked at me like I was an idiot," the old man had said, detaining Rick in the foyer of his rent-controlled apartment.

"Pathetic old queen," Buzz had hissed as he pushed his way out the door to the street.

Fuck him. Thank God for capitalism. Buzz had realized it would be money that determined his suitability, again, and he'd turned angrily into the pet shop just steps away. This time, the needy, pleading looks of the gentler puppy-mill spawn had been only vile to him, and the little snapping pinscher had seemed to perfectly suit his mood. One thing, though, had irked him almost as much as the previous demand for personality-based petworthiness, and that was, that there were no full-length mirrors in the shop where he could view himself as he was trying them on. How the fuck was he supposed to see how he looked with various breeds and sizes? As if everyone, especially these fags on Christopher, didn't know that most dogs were bought as dick-magnets, and that cruising men were as discriminating and judgmental in their choice of pup-with-man-package as they were with a potential prospect sallying down the West Village streets. Really, dogs could now be seen as the 21st Century equivalent of the kerchief-in-the-back-pockets of the 1970's – just as good a way to signal -– top, bottom, leather, only gives oral, only receives oral, will never allow himself to be fucked, turned on by narcolepsy, S/ M, etc. etc. etc., for gay men were nothing if not specific about their desires to an astonishing degree.

And equating the two codes had been his newest stroke of genius. For as his father ranted on and on about the need for this project

Buzz made his entrance replete with his newest purchase: a hyper-active miniature pinscher that growled and darted maniacally at each human being within reach.

to be completed ASAP and Flynn listened intently and occasionally twitched his leg away from the diminutive circling beast, Buzz let his imagination run rampant – different collars and leashes for the dogs and maybe even ear piercings or doggie outfits that could be used as ever more specific communications of desire.

There was a big-ass fly in this ointment, however, and that was that he was already tiring of the constant responsibility of having a dog at all, and found himself wishing he could just check it in a coatroom or hand it to a doggie-valet. The "no dogs allowed" signs of stores and restaurants that had made him and his friends laugh, as young discriminating gays who considered themselves of above average attractiveness, were now no longer funny. Once you actually owned a dog, you no longer appreciated its double meaning.

And yet his new addition had already become invaluable for attracting tricks. The pinscher, with its aggressive attitude and small but seriously off-putting bark, was proving to be quite valuable. Buzz had already gotten blow-jobs from two self-hating submissives, one of whom had wanted to involve the dog, and Buzz had experienced great pleasure in denying him that request - that was an added bonus. It – for he hadn't come up with a name yet – also kept away the kind of people Buzz wanted to avoid and by whom owners with different, more cuddlyfuzzy breeds were perpetually victimized. Mothers with toddlers in tow, desperately seeking distractions, for example. "Can I pet him, mommy?" wouldn't even have a chance of developing thanks to the bared fangs, and, another demographic, single women, wouldn't fawn over the thing and block Buzz's path to coo "ooohh- so cute!" and have their unwanted attention get in the way of his access to a fast-moving cruise.

"BUZZ!"

"Dad?"

"Get that little bastard off my desk." The animal had leapt up in front of Harry and was leaning forward at a 45 degree angle as if readying itself for a lunge. "Were you goddamn listening to anything at all?"

"Of course, Dad." Buzz gave a small, cursory tug on the two-hundred and fifty dollar leash, and the Min Pin spun around and bared his teeth. Buzz did likewise and his new pet started back in surprise, then jumped to the floor and began his manic, random circling all over again.

"Good boy," said Buzz.

"Well?" said Harry.

"Oh, definitely," said Buzz.

"Just don't fuck it up this time."

"And 'it' would be?"

"Good God, why did I ever fucking have a son?" Harry turned to Flynn. "You talk to him. I'm done." He got up and walked out.

Flynn took a deep breath.

"He was telling you, you need to go to Provincetown and track down Sally for a final offer."

"Who?"

"You know. Sally. The woman who owns Aunt Muffin's."

Buzz wrinkled his nose. "No way. Ugh. Provincetown smells like fish."

"Well… it is right on the ocean."

Buzz rolled his eyes. "Not *that* kind of fish. Anyway, I've got deals. Things to do. I won't be around. Tell him to send one of those flunkies that sits out front. Yeah," he laughed. "And you can tell them there's more pussy there than in their wildest dreams. That should get them going. Not that they'll get any of it." He laughed again, got up, and dragged his dog out of the room behind him. He managed to evade his father, who was standing with his back to the him, looking out the plate glass window.

Harry didn't notice his son leaving. He was evaluating several massive buildings in the distance. None had the proximity to the park that his did. What a triumph that was! Beat that, Hollywood, he thought, but he knew that it was nonsensical to compare getting a development done in New York City to getting a movie made. Or was it? It was just as difficult, if not more so. It was just that here the cast of characters was completely different. It too was based on obscene amounts of money and cronyism but egos were not as involved. Few developers save the hairpiece guy needed the constant infusion of attention that was par for the course on the West Coast. There were mercifully few "stars" in this profession. Name recognition on a grand scale wasn't important, in fact, it was the average developer's nightmare to see his name in the papers. Those rag-tag bunches of anarchists that appeared like fruit flies around the juicy smell of a neighborhood ripe for devouring liked to make it personal these days. While producers and directors collected accolades the bigger their movies were, the bigger the developer became, the bigger target he was. Luckily in most cases, the "opposition," if you could even call it that, was about as lightweight and easily batted away as the aforementioned flying insects, and the campaigns they waged had about as long a life as did the little buggers. They really weren't fair fights at all, thought Harry. He was a self-made man in many respects; he had a memory of being the underdog.

He inspected his cell for signs of missed messages from Mrs. H. She had interrupted the launch of his VIP phone marathon, but he was too enamored now to resent it. What a wonderful lunch they'd had! They'd only chatted superficially but the amount of attention she'd shown him and the genuine interest she seemed to take in his projects had left him almost levitating off the ground. Would she be getting in touch with him soon? In an effort to advance their acquaintance he had offered to take her on a touristy tour of the surrounding area, and she had accepted with gracious enthusiasm. What a far cry from his first wife, who, like many women who marry a man primarily for his money, was perpetually bored and dissatisfied and a back seat driver whenever she roused herself from her prone position in the back seat. She'd periodically raise her Gucci sunglasses and take a peek at whatever road-sign of their life's direction they were currently passing. "Do we really wanna go there?" she'd groan, before lowering her shades and laying back down. It didn't much matter where "there" was, the important thing was the objection itself.

Harry's eyes fell on the lush green of Prospect Park. Should they take a nature drive to start? Then - a drink at the Marriot, and a ride down Fourth Avenue, where he'd casually gesture to the newest block of his condos that couldn't fail to impress, then perhaps take her to the mall on Atlantic in case she needed to shop. Women liked these things. His first wife could never relax unless she knew they were within twenty minutes of a mall at any time. Then dinner at the River Café, whose owners only owed him ten or twelve favors. After that they could have a walk on the Brooklyn Heights Promenade.

All set, if in fact she ever got in touch as she had promised. Harry sighed and turned away from the window, pushing Helen out of his mind and resuming his musings on the unhappy fate that awaited the vast majority of those who dared to stand in the way of powerful interests in

New York City. Crushed like bugs, indeed. It was almost sad to see their pathetic efforts as they went up against the phalanxes of lawyers who moved like an unstoppable advancing army towards victory. The developers' machine was just too well funded, the tactics so tried and true, honed from years of skirmishes, each lesson learned and incorporated into future strategies. There were endless reinforcements available made possible by vast resources. There was no burnout for their side, no conflict between making a living and the numerous weeks, months, or years required to make a difference, no need to weigh the wisdom of taking on the role of David in a city full of Goliaths.

Those little groups who did hold their ground found themselves like surrounded Indians, their flimsy arrows pointed at gun barrels, holding on to their hope in the fairness of the American people like an outdated belief in the Great Spirit. Their mouthpieces thought they were the shamans of justice, but these days, the centuries-old American advancement towards egalitarianism had been slowed to a glacial pace, if not altogether eradicated. The rights of the individual were starting to melt away just like the edges of the great blocks of ice. It was disturbing as a whole, except when applied to his own gain.

Like most people, Harry's true political party was the Me Party. Take the recent court decisions on the legality of eminent domain and the subsequent applications of the ruling in its favor! What could be better than that! The ecstasy of the continually expanding definition of the word "public" and the joy corporate lawyers would have digging into that for future use and racking up billable hours!

Yes, the development industry had recovered brilliantly since their most humiliating defeat – when decades ago that little commie woman rallied the troops in the West Village and blocked a key artery in Robert Moses' takeover and makeover of numerous small neighborhoods into highways and high rise projects from the Bronx to Brooklyn. Of course, the properties he hadn't been able to touch were now worth a fortune...go figure.

"Mr. Harmony?"

Harry turned from his musings to see Flynn. Harry noticed that his employee was sporting a somewhat questionable shoulder bag. He peered closer.

"Hey, is that a skyline?" he said.

"I don't think so," said Flynn.

"Very creative," said Harry. "Get me one. I'll reimburse you. What's up?"

"Uh, Buzz won't be able to make it to Provincetown. He said he had other plans. I would go but –"

"Hold on. What time is it?"

"Oh." Flynn pulled out his phone. "Six-thirty."

Helen was not going to call.

"Fuck it," said Harry to Flynn. "Every day we put this on hold it's costing me shitloads. You said Buzz already had a meeting, right? Who's gonna say we didn't give it our best shot?"

"No doubt," said Flynn, realizing it was a rhetorical question.

"What's that?" said Harry. Flynn had stuffed that day's newspapers under his arm.

"Oh. Just a couple – articles about that uh, movie star's disappearance. Not that I care."

Harry nodded sagely. "Old publicity trick," he said. "Ten to one the studio's behind it. Trust me. Half the terminal diseases you hear about are too. That and the romances for the guys who never went coed. Never underestimate how low those bloodsuckers will go to sell a picture."

"Really?" said Flynn.

"The reporters lap it up like anteaters at a bug-infested honey jar. Christ. Just what we need. Now they'll be crawling all over here trying to snort up a story like pornographers on a three-day coke binge. Poking their powder – covered noses into every corner of the neighborhood they think they can sniff into a scoop."

"Couldn't it be good, though, in a way?" said Flynn. "I mean, it'll distract them from what's going on the site, right?"

"You're absolutely fucking right!" Harry paused in his rant. "Come to think of it, with all the missing cleavage they're gonna splash all over the front page from here til doomsday, who the fuck is gonna care about some eyesore and a bunch of building-huggers clinging to it like it's a goddamn redwood? You're absolutely right. It'll be the perfect distraction, the tits on that woman, dead or alive, once we start swinging that crane."

* * *

Nicole descended into depths of the West Fourth Street subway station, where she was hit with the usual wave of hot and foul-smelling air. She was tired. It had been a long day of the daily grind, literally. There were worse jobs, she reminded herself, as she began the interminable wait for the "F" train. There was the intoxicating aroma of freshly roasted coffees; the dedicated patrons; the old store itself, with its charming vintage interior. The regulars coming in for their fix; the seekers on a pilgrimage to find the epic cup.

True, there were customers, more and more each day, who radiated the impatience and anxiety of those who had no true need of anything, and so believed they had to have everything without delay. Delving into one huge burlap bag after another, scooping up the exotic beans for inspection for a couple whose laser-like stares followed her every move, she'd had to admit to herself that she was over it. It was the hated truth: she was getting too old for this. She could no longer perform her duties with the grace and perky smile she'd brought to it just a couple of years earlier. It only got more grueling as you went through the same motions for the ten thousandth time, and soon your good-will and enthusiasm was replaced by a mask-like determination to just get through 'til the next break.

Her friends that had been numerous in the neighborhood from various art scenes or schools had all moved on; they no longer stopped by to brighten her day and remind her of the reason she kept this menial job. Sleep, paint, coffee, repeat. It had all worked together in a carefully protective way. It let her avoid the mass ugliness of midtown, and it took her straight from her studio to an area of the city where there were still small winding streets and legendary clubs, even if the hideousness of Sixth Avenue couldn't be circumvented entirely. There was still a trace of transgression that couldn't be fully eradicated, still adventurous kids from the suburbs who ventured down fresh off the Penn Station or Port Authority boat for some stolen fun or because they'd heard this was a place where it was still okay to be different.

There were people who worked in the store who came in for their shifts already exhausted before even beginning the day, full of a crappy vibe, people who had worked there for too many years, who hated

116

their small salaries that were impossible to live on, and spent their breaks smoking cigarettes, sucking the poisonous fumes deep into their lungs, staring out into the air full of a generalized disappointment. It was Nicole's biggest fear that she'd end up like that, too deadened to even bitch anymore about the lack of cheap rents or the ridiculous commute they'd been forced into since the only place they could now afford to live was someplace like Brighton Beach or Bushwick, or, for fuck's sake, Bedford–Stuyvesant, and even the latter, once even more infamous and deadly than the South Bronx back in the day, was, impossibly, becoming gentrified.

Of the artists she knew, those who were still trying to make it in the City were an ever-dwindling minority; for one, if they were painters, chances were they no longer had spaces to work in. They'd long ago been converted to upscale housing for the rich who'd wanted to live in an artistic area. The musicians' gigs, meanwhile, were few and far between. In place of the instruments they once carried, they now lugged around a New York City brand of sunken bitterness borne of decades of struggle, and were just downright scary, with their frozen-in-time belief that at forty-five, fame was still just around the corner, their belittling of others they'd known that had "made it," and their rage that they had so far not been given the due that was clearly their birthright.

When she took her fifteen minutes, she could see even more destroyed human beings, various relics asleep and/or dead drunk in the little square in the middle of Bleecker and Sixth, the filth of their clothes, their rough, weathered skin, the dreams of their youth in invisible piles next to them on the benches where they slept, still clearer and more real to them than the reality of the situation in which they now found themselves.

But I don't have any dreams, Nicole told herself as the train finally pulled in, *I don't have any dreams so I can't ever be like them.*

Out on Seventh Avenue, she felt just how nervous she was about seeing Flynn that night. He was just so damn good-looking, and he seemed so, well, normal, really, compared with the guys she usually ended up with. It was like – there was no sarcasm, no seductive posturing followed by distance, no attempt to manipulate her with the tried-and-true method employed by insecure boys of alternating compliments and put-downs. It seemed completely unlikely that he was the type who would display the weird combination of worship and neglect to which she had become accustomed.

Then there was Ned. Of course. Ned, Ned, Ned. She'd wanted to break up with him forever. He'd been such a jerk when she called him about the window. It was so typical. He was so selfish. The kind of guy who left his dirty pants and socks lying around her apartment when he stayed over. The kind of guy who would take the last beer out of the fridge without asking anyone else if they wanted it. The kind of guy who let his lecherous eye wander uninhibited over little-girl-dressed fans of the bands he followed, even when Nicole was standing right next to him. What a jerk, thought Nicole.

Time was getting slim. It was already past seven. But it'd be cool. She'd get home and pick out one of her favorite vintage gowns and maybe even take a risk and pin one side of her hair back with an eye-catching barrette. Slip her feet into those cheap but cute Chinatown Mary-Jane shoes.

It never took her very long to get dressed to go out. But it had been a long time since she had dressed up to stay *in*. Stayed in for someone she had a really, really big crush on.

I'm such a jerk, thought Nicole, I'm such a jerk for thinking he could ever like me.

She looked breathtakingly beautiful. That's what Flynn thought when Nicole opened the downstairs door and he saw her standing there with her pale lilac gown that became lace on the top part of her breasts.

She wasn't perfectly pretty like Constance, she didn't have model-like features that supposedly defined beauty, but that was the whole point: it was *her* face particularly that he liked. He felt way more excited looking at her than he had looking at the women that had been considered head-turners in the financial district. Her lips were soft and full and she was shorter than him in a way that was just right, and she was very, very nicely curved.

"Wow. Great dress!"

"Street find," Nicole cut in, in a flat, unattractive voice. "Look, it's torn over here. I always wear old stuff," she prattled on. "I just like it so much better than the crap they make now, you know? It's like the

118

Gap, it's ruined everything." With this charming introduction she proceeded up the stairs, then paused before the door to her apartment.

"I know you're just going to go up to the roof to fix it but, I thought, maybe you'd want to hang out like, you know, for like a minute first? I mean, it's so nice of you to fix it, so, would you like some wine or something?"

"Absolutely. Thanks."

Nicole led Flynn into her apartment.

Nice. That was the first thing he thought as he looked around. Way more homey than the studio, although that wouldn't be hard. Cute little table by the kitchen area. Nice big bed – that never hurt - carpets on the floor…

"Wow," he said, and then thought how stupid that sounded.

Nicole came towards him with two glasses of wine in ornate goblets, both of which were slightly damaged. "Sorry about these," she said. "I found them in a box on the street and they were so pretty."

"Not at all." He took one and sipped it carefully, avoiding the chip on the rim. His eyes scanned the walls – plenty of paintings here, but nothing like the ones he'd seen before.

"These are yours, too, right?"

"Yup. I paint down there a lot. The Gowanus."

"Wow, these are really great." He'd said "wow" again? How had that happened?

"Thanks." Nicole took a large gulp of her wine, and a couple of crimson droplets fell down onto her chest.

Flynn couldn't help but follow their progress quite closely. Out of the corner of his eye he saw Nicole arresting the trickle into her cleavage and licking the wine from her ring finger. "Very, very cool," he said, and wrenched his eyes away to look at the view from the Union Street Bridge. "So – where's the bird crap?"

"Oh. Well. That was just one idea. And you can't say it's not relevant."

"Right," said Flynn. "You had a lot of ideas about that."

"I know. Anyway," she continued, going to sit down on her loveseat, "I know your clients don't want that stuff. But they probably wouldn't want this either, right? It's not 'arty' enough. It's not in-your-face. Nobody knows my name."

"I - don't know about that." The less he said the better. He hated having to lie.

"Okay, I'll give you a deal. Four of these," she pointed at the landscapes, "for half price, BUT, you gotta take all the shitty ones too."

"Funny," said Flynn, grinning and coming over to sit next to her.

He was close. Very close. And he was wearing a tie. It was unbearably sexy. She'd never had sex with a guy who wore a tie before. She wanted to grab it and pull him down on top of her.

"Anyway," she said, returning to the safe realm of her opinions, "what's the point of making art if you're not going to *say* something. So what if I can't sell anything? I'm used to it."

"Must be rough, sometimes, though," said Flynn. He finished his glass and put it on the floor.

"I guess so." She didn't want to admit it. "Most of my friends have given up."

"And you? Why haven't you?"

Where the fuck was the wine bottle? She needed more wine *now*. "I don't know what I'd do. If I didn't do it, you know? Like, Iggy said, if he wasn't into music, he'd probably be in jail."

"Can't your parents help you?"

Nicole raised her eyebrows. "You don't know many artists, do you?"

"Why don't I get up there and fix the roof," said Flynn.

He climbed up the ladder behind Nicole. Despite the respectful distance he'd kept from her, so far, he couldn't ignore what was just above him. He was all for feminism and what not, but was he really supposed to not look at that? She had a completely different kind of sway to her hips, than, say, someone like Dale. It wasn't at all calculated. Some women were just built that way. He grinned to himself. It was conceivable that any minute now her dress could just rip all the way down the back. Guiltily, he pulled himself up the last rung.

He knelt down and began to take the brushes and sealant out of the bag. He was glad he'd finally found a legitimate use for it.

"*Interesting bag*," said Nicole, with a smirk.

"Well, it's kinda new," said Flynn defensively.

"Hey, I thought you were an art dealer. Do you always carry around household repair items?"

She watched as he rolled up his sleeves.

"You know, you really are … kind of weird for an art guy. I mean, you're not gay…" she let her words trail off on purpose.

"Right," said Flynn, without looking up.

"Plus, you didn't hate my paintings."

"Well, I did find the Gowanus ones more likeable, for some odd reason."

They both laughed.

"Why don't I go down and bring up the rest of the wine," said Nicole.

Downstairs she went straight for the mirror. Was the barrette working? Wearing her hair over one eye was a holdover from her teenage years, when everyone had their personal bit of fashion business they were convinced was the only thing saving them from hideous ugliness, and at the same time, made them look incredibly sexy. She unclipped the barrette. At least she no longer woke up wearing eyeliner.

Flynn was just finishing up when she returned to the roof.

"That should do it," he said, standing up and wiping the dirt from his hands.

"Here." She held out his glass.

"It really is gorgeous up here," he said.

"I know," said Nicole.

"Cheers." They clinked glasses.

"Nice tie," said Nicole.

CHAPTER SIX

They hadn't ended up sleeping together, but what *had* happened, was a couple of slow, deep kisses, hours later, after they'd talked into the night. About pretty much everything. Except bands.

The next morning, as she lay in bed, she couldn't think of anything else. His face, his eyes, his hair. How he kissed her. Easy, but hard. In short, he was a man, not a boy. A man to make a nun rip a hole in her habit, as Raymond Chandler might have said, had he ever written from the woman's point of view.

Can I see you again? Soon? he'd asked. How about Saturday, and Ned had flashed across Nicole's mind for an instant. But Saturdays were like Tuesdays now for the couple, and they never saw each other on Tuesdays anymore.

Plus, thought Nicole, getting up and beginning her coffee ritual, the "Weevils' Business" had infested every aspect of Ned's life and was always put first now. Ned was certain that the founder, Fredericke, had the same level or greater of integrity as Kurt Cobain, which could mean terminal obscurity, or, played right, the exact opposite. He'd let her know he needed to keep an ever watchful eye on the fluctuations of the market for what he believed was his high-risk but potentially blue-chip stock. He had to be able to capitalize at a moment's notice on every event that could possibly relate to the Weevils' mission statement.

Nicole had once had a dream where Ned had taken a call from Rolling Stone while they were exchanging wedding vows.

So, with a deep lack of guilt, she had said yes to Flynn.

She went downstairs to get milk for her coffee. When she went outside, she again experienced the culture shock of the changing neighborhood. Apparently she'd gone to sleep in Brooklyn and woken up in Norway. How did all of these children get to be so white and blond? As she paid for her groceries she contemplated the future of this generation. Some people said there'd be a big wake-up call for this particular breed, that once they got older they'd have a sharp awakening to the fact that the world didn't revolve around them. She didn't agree. In her opinion, which was of course the truth, they would be wrapped for

*Apparently she had gone to sleep in Brooklyn
and woken up in Norway.*

life in the big cocoon of their total self-involvement which would inflate to epic proportions like an air-bag at any potential crash into so-called "reality." Which was really what, by the way? A world that would welcome, not reject, their monstrous egos. A society that would fit them like the other piece of the fucked-up puzzle. There was no widespread moral code anymore, there was no reward for such outdated attributes as "virtue" and "generosity," let alone the forgotten concept of "integrity," and the now widely dismissed value of one's "soul." It was as if the previously prized, nay, venerated-above-all, spiritual possessions of mankind had never even existed. Prizes and possessions were now strictly material, and apparently, no one had noticed the change. Why should they, when gift-cards for the Gap were available at every gas station, when credit was more common than courtesy? Sharing what you had just left you poorer, not appreciated. Things had flipped inside out, the most selfish behavior was the most rewarded, the so-called minorities, whether they were women or people of color, were once again spreading their legs or tap-dancing their way in various obvious or disguised ways to wealth or fame, while those who objected were dubbed "haters," or defused by being declared to be "just jealous." The little kids were being groomed to be a reflection of these types who were idolized: famous figures whose blow-fish-like personalities were admired both for their puffiness and for their off-putting spikes. It was these evolutionary traits that were winning out, leaving previous developments such as the brief foray into humanity dwindling like a once-employed vestigial tail. "Nicky, it's not even noon." She heard Ned's voice in her head, criticizing her for yet again mentally taking on the world at inappropriate moments. Hypocrite, she thought. As if investing alternative rock bands with religious power and magnifying their importance to mythological proportions was somehow less neurotic; a sainted mission. At least she didn't smoke pot to turn it off, like he did.

Her eyes swept over the magazines at the newsstand. The usual parade of desperate blondes on the covers of celebrity and "women's magazines," the sports figures, cars, guns, and hip-hop felons, and the latest successful rock bands, and then she saw BORECORE: MEET THE LITTLE WEEVILS p. 36, right on the front of one of the music weeklies.

What? Why hadn't Ned told her this was happening? She grabbed the paper. He'd always been over-eager to share his maniacal tracking of the band's progress. She opened it up. There were two and a half columns, no less, and a photo of the band crammed together with their hair and beards taking up most of the picture, looking intently into the camera as if transmitting secret alternative messages to their fans, and Dingle magazine, based in Austin, Texas, had a wide and growing circulation and was even generally thought of as an über-underground Rolling Stone.

She scanned the article and was quickly put off by the use of certain words: "trope,""public and private space," "conflate," terms such as these evoked a deep joy in her that she had not gone to grad school. How this journalist – a "Brenda James," had managed to work them into an article about six young men who were happiest simply banging their cans was beyond her; even Ned would have balked at lifting these valued signifiers from the treasure trove of unpublished theses and placing them in the crown of his criticism unaltered.

"Borecore" it seemed, was the writer's clever way of coining yet another "core" phrase, meant ironically *of course*; it was the jumping off point for a lengthy exposition on how their unflinching honesty functioned to bore through the sell-out world of mainstream music which she compared to a sack of old flour. Needless to say, they were the *opposite* of boring.

How pretentious! But of course Ned would love this. *This woman would be the perfect match for him*, Nicole thought sarcastically. She was surprised to see that he had been interviewed as well, and was quoted issuing similarly inflated pronouncements decipherable only by academics, and it came to her that since he had told her nothing about this, perhaps he had had the very same idea.

She saw that the front door of Aunt Muffin's was open. Maybe now was a good time to talk to Sally about the lights and the window.

She stepped inside.

"Hello?" she called out.

There was no answer.

"Sally? Wendy?" The back door was open. She could see that it had suddenly got darker outside. Clouds were appearing across the sky and a wind was making the leaves sway.

She walked cautiously down the steps to the patio.

"Hello?" There were traces of a barbecue and tattered streamers, but nothing else.

A hand grasped her below the elbow.

Nicole jumped. "Holy shit!!!! God, Pat! You nearly gave me a heart attack." It was Pat, Sally's partner, who had come up behind her in her wheelchair.

"Sorry. I was gonna call up to you but I was winded from the ramp."

"Ramp? What ramp?"

"Sally put one in so I could get up and down from the basement."

"The basement?"

"She didn't tell you? We're living down there now."

"What?"

"Gave up our apartment. Had to. If we wanna save this place, we're gonna have legal fees. Big ones."

"Shit," said Nicole. "But how do you –"

"Get around in my wheelchair?" Pat finished for her. "I can't get everywhere right now. But Sally's going to fix it up. Lucia and Regina bring me stuff. It's okay. Sally's getting back soon."

"But the front door was open."

"Was it? Oh, it was probably one of the girls. Sometimes they come in early to get the cleaning started."

"But there wasn't – "

"Was there something you needed?"

"Oh, it's cool. It can wait." She felt like an ass being so paranoid. Look what Pat had to deal with every day. Real bullshit.

Whilst she engaged in the alchemical ritual that would transform ordinary water and beans into the sacred draught with the magical power to get her through the day, Nicole began to plan her date with Flynn. They would start the evening with the dinner she would prepare: Italian, because she could in fact make a mean spaghetti sauce, but she would keep it as light as possible so that they both wouldn't feel weighed down. Not that they were necessarily going to have sex, although she had already thought of it in quite some detail a few times, but still, you never wanted to get too sleepy after eating mounds of carbohydrates. There was no marathon to be run the next day. No garlic bread, that was for sure, although she did love the way the hot seasoned crunch combined with the melted butter.

It would be hard to find the authentic ingredients now that the little family-owned Italian store that had been four blocks away and stocked imported canned tomatoes, olive oils, its own fresh-made pasta and bread and slabs of Parmesan and Romano cheese ready to be grated fresh for each customer (pre-grated cheese, like pre-packaged mozzarella, would never disgrace their shelves) had gone under due to a quadrupled rent, and had been replaced with a cell-phone chain store. She might actually have to go to the one on West Houston Street which had survived due to God's grace or more likely because it was owned by an old Italian family. For him only, she'd venture to Manhattan. It wouldn't hurt to show him that she could cook really, really well. She froze as she was about to add the hot milk to the coffee. *WHAT THE FUCK IS HAPPENING TO ME????* *The thought was practically prehistoric!*

Whatever. She'd better check out the fridge. There was Ned's last artisanal beer which he had rushed to buy after reading about it in a so-called "foodie" magazine. It was brewed in Brooklyn with hops imported from the East side of the Northern-most area in Wales and apricots grown in the Hamptons, or some such pretentious bullshit. It was made in the far reaches of hipster Greenpoint or Williamsburg by a bunch of guys who had seemed to Ned to be just like him, only with more money.

Nicole grabbed it and emptied it down the sink. *This one's for the homie that ain't here.* Thank God.

Saturday was approaching far faster than Flynn would have liked. As much as he was anticipating seeing Nicole again, he dreaded it because of his deception. And he had more on his plate now: his father had just phoned him with another request to help out one of his friends. As the economy had continued to sour, it had become more and more common for his dad to dole out promises that his son would offer expert financial advice gratis.

"Don't worry about it," he'd say over their protests, "Your money's no good here."

Of course their money would have been quite good, but there was no doubt that the firemen, construction workers and army buddies desperately needed his help. Most of them were constantly struggling with the confusion of keeping their families afloat in the riptide currents of New York's financial waters. The swirling seas were full of prehistoric-sized serpents seeking to swallow their pensions whole or decimate their numbers due to city budget cuts.

Flynn often found himself pained by the way the men approached their problems: their lack of self-pity, their commitment to their jobs and their desire just to hold onto what was in fact hardly sufficient remuneration in the first place for the dangerous and oftentimes deadly jobs they performed. In the last several years he'd been more and more dismayed by the discrepancies between the rewards top Wall Streeters regularly received as compared to the pittances thrown to the men who literally put their lives on the line. Fifty million dollars for one year's bonus for men whose biggest personal risk was a heart attack from too many straight scotches and rare steaks? Who sat on their considerable asses day after day lifting nothing heavier than the confidential files of their biggest investors?

But what could he do about it? Back when he'd worked in finance, the last thing on his mind was biting the hand that fed him. So he'd tried to make it up to them as best he could, going over their individual circumstances, looking at tax returns and mortgage bills and the dwindling resources of those who were regularly lauded as being the city's finest in every way save equivalent compensation.

Today's problem was the disarray of a retired firefighter's finances. "He's a good guy, he just made some mistakes," said his father. "Oh, and Flanagan says thank you. He says you saved his ass. From his wife, at least."

"Sure, Dad, I'll talk to him."

"Should I have him call you, or what?"

"Of course," said Flynn, wondering why it was that his father asked him that every single time.

"Okay, good. I just don't want him calling up and you don't know who he is."

"Dad, I remember him from when I was a kid. I remember all those guys."

"Okay, good. Thanks, I'll tell him. Sean O'Connor. Just so you don't forget."

"I know, Dad. Sure. Anytime."

"Susan wants to go shopping so I have to go."

"Okay."

"Son."

"Yes, Dad?"

"You turned out pretty good, you know that? You're like your grandfather. He was a stand-up guy too."

Buzz sat back in his club chair and took another swig of his drink. His fucking bank account was still fucking sub-par. Doug Holmes had finally called him, the dipshit, and produced a volley of financial facts that in Buzz's mind, amounted to accusations, as if he, BUZZ, was somehow responsible for the mess.

Yeah, of course, he'd been the one to actually spend the money, but it was Holmes' job to make sure the dregs were caught in the strainer of his financial wizardry, patching up problems, transferring funds, selling stock, doing whatever.

But Buzz was too smart to start a barrage of yelling over the phone; in his mind, cursing out your banker and letting him know what a loser scumbag he was, was akin to insulting your waiter just before he returned to the kitchen to fetch your entrée. No use pissing in your own pool, especially if you were prone to swimming in such a way as to stir up the waters.

There was no getting around the fact that he was in continued deep shit. The payments he'd received from working for the so-far faceless person or persons who had hired him to throw a wrench in the works at the Aunt Muffin's meeting, although quite handsome, didn't put enough of a dent in his debts, and more importantly, didn't clear the road to his ultimate goal – the acquisition of the still-on-the-market dream apartment that he continued to stalk online night and day.

At first he'd been gung-ho about engaging in a fresh bout of activities that would annoy and possibly completely fuck over his father, but he was already tiring of the balance of power within this new "relationship." He'd been surprised when he'd been contacted by the anonymous caller, who refused to be identified, and then he'd never been dealt with in quite this way before: nothing more than a few words communicated against an absolutely silent background. In some basic, primal way he knew that there was only one way to respond, and that was in absolute agreement, arguments silenced, comments abandoned, terms accepted nearly instantaneously. Actually, it had been more of a command than a job offer. There was no negotiation about money, even. "You'll get paid," was the full extent of the exchange on that subject. There were all different kinds of silence, he was discovering, and this one wasn't one he ever wanted to hear again.

His vicious little Min Pin startled him out of his reverie by letting out a yap that showed the back of its throat and the full rows of his upper and lower pointy yellowish white teeth. He glared at Buzz and then stood on his hind legs and stuck his long nose directly down into Buzz's scotch.

"You little – shit! I'll leash you!" cried Buzz, jumping up, but it dashed to safety and turned around to face Buzz with what appeared to him to be a nasty and challenging grin, then settled itself on a generously proportioned maroon leather armchair and sniffed at its antiqued brass tacks.

Buzz strode angrily towards the hall closet, then had a second thought and made for his bedroom, where he dove beneath his king-sized bed and pulled out a large black box. Throwing off the lid he viewed its contents: the accoutrements of various past and future S/ M encounters: all manner of cuffs, restraints, black hoods, paddles, etc.

Ah. Here it was! He drew out the muzzle, but it was all wrong, and Buzz threw it back in the box in disgust. His dog's snout was long and slender, it would never fit as it might have had he been say, a boxer or bullmastiff, some of whose faces were so human it was downright frightening.

Furious, he strode out onto his terrace to ease his frustration by focusing his wrath at the usual targets: other gay men in Chelsea. There went a teenager wearing drain-pipe black trousers and pointy Beatle-style boots. Ugh, thought Buzz, probably listens to English bands and goes to Irving Plaza. When he was fifteen these little queer types had already provoked his contempt, and here they still were, an affront to the fashion world and all those who sought out Chelsea as a place to find an acceptable fuck. There went the muscle queens on their way to the gym. Some of the gyms would have done well to put up a velvet rope like their nighttime brethren. In fact, all of Chelsea should have such a rope, perhaps all of Manhattan. Then there were the prancing the-only-word-for-them-could-ever-be-fags types, and now they all had their diminutive doggies, and it annoyed the fuck out of Buzz to see their happy little breeds, waving their soft tails back and forth like little flags announcing their asses were available underneath. The dogs, not the men – but how perfect, really. Why not just stick a fucking tail on yourself? he thought angrily, as he watched the chatting and flirting of the boys whose pets ran to each other like Romeos and Juliets kept apart by the dueling families of man and beast, straining at their leashes, sniffing each others' behinds (that would be a timesaver for men), sprawling on their backs and occasionally licking each other's balls or more often where they had been, to the barely masked delight of the owners.

By contrast there was his own super snarky advance guard. Little bastard. If only he could have a different dog whenever he wanted. This one was perfect for taking a stroll in the dwindling vestiges of dark and forbidden places near the last remains of blacked-out windows and boarded-up doorways. He went well with particular types of men, sex act/s, and locations, but what if the snarling chased away a different kind of trick? He should just be able to trade him in, at least for the night. He could see it now: A pooch for every party. A dog for every doggy-style. Like a fucking Zipcar, but with pets.

Buzz strode back into his apartment. There sat his current accessory, now, in his mind, like yesterday's fashion, like a drag-queen's dress bought for that girl's night out and returned the next day, to the knowing disgust of savvy salespersons at certain large-sized ladies' stores.

"I might go out to a different club tonight, how would you like that?" he said. "A different pooch might be waiting for me at the curb outside of it. Maybe a poodle that knows what's what. "

He strode into the next room and looked at himself in a huge mirror with a dark wood frame from Restoration Hardware that leaned against the wall. Unexpectedly, his still-unnamed dog came and sat rapt by Buzz's pants leg, mimicking his master by staring back at its own likeness.

"Hmmph," Buzz sniffed, trying not to be impressed.

Then it came to him in a flash. His own company that he would take public and that would solve the problem not only of his expanding debt, but also the lack of full-length mirrors in pet stores: Zoomdog ™ .

Chapter Seven

The sun was shining on Saturday but Nicole's internal barometer had readjusted itself since that morning after, and was now back to floating between dark clouds and high pressure.

It was all a mistake, Flynn didn't really like her, she had nothing to say to him, they were too different.

She ran water for a bath. The claw-foot tub was in the kitchen. They must have had to heat the water up and pour it in right from the stove. Soaking in the tub, she closed her eyes and imagined a huge pot boiling on an ancient source of heat, a woman heaving it up by herself and dumping the water in, the whole family bathing in it one after another. Living by herself but still requiring privacy, she'd put up Japanese screens and hung a Chinese paper lamp overhead. She'd draped the cord around the exposed pipe that ran the length of the apartment and had been used for God knows what God knows when. She knew that the whole thing could just fall down one day. Risky, maybe. Some people might even say she had a death wish. How many artists does it take to screw in a light bulb over a tub of water? Just one, electrocuting herself at the height of her creativity, receiving notoriety and recognition only after her death, the act itself to be deconstructed and discussed ad infinitum, opinions offered as to whether it was accident or suicide as performance, and because she was a woman, her assumed despondency to be attributed to the lack of a man in her life… She slid down deeper into the water, her dark hair floating up and around her face.

What fucking bullshit this all was. Death, taxes, men, fucked up rent, all inevitable. For example, the death knell of what she had loved sounded by the arrival of those who walked their large dogs languidly in flip-flops in the South Slope, talking about their stocks and ideas. You could always tell someone who wasn't a native New Yorker because someone born in Manhattan would never, ever wear flip-flops on the street. It was a surefire way to spot a transfer from Boulder or Northern California or maybe Seattle. She had never been to Seattle but had gotten the impression that even though people were pumped with rich, dark roasts, consumed morning, noon and night, it was somehow still a laid-back place where locals strolled unconcernedly over pristine sidewalks near unlocked bicycles. It had taken a while after the arrival of the first few of these filth-oblivious beings to begin to make sense of their alien lifestyle and their über-relaxed state, and then, one day, in a flash of obviousness, it occurred to her that they had money. Lots of it. And so she had decoded the DNA of their definition of "chill."

Then, the constant guilty feeling that she was deliberately being a fuck-off and irresponsibly wasting her time. The constant nagging question of when you were going to get a real CAREER and a real JOB and harness yourself to debt, mortgages, and days filled with a thousand and one duties that you hated, this allegedly meaning you had finally "grown up."

She sank down further until the water completely covered her face. The dramatic declaration of Jim Morrison played back in her head:

"This is the end…"

She sat up and gasped for breath. It was a good thing she'd never been a hippie. Flower children just got mowed down.

Dinner at her house. In the male world, that was code for You Are Going to Get Laid. Everyone knew that when a woman went to the trouble of actually cooking a meal for you she is seriously offering you more than just food. The low lights, the lingering meal, the wine… and then ending up in bed. He'd done it before. But with Nicole, it felt different. She was so unpredictable. That was good, but also, a little scary.

Flynn opened his bedroom door and was finally able to decode the blast of repeating sounds that had been banging through his walls for what seemed like hours.

"Kashmir?" Looped? Really?

He flicked on the TV super-loud and flipped through the channels. He'd kept an almost unwilling eye on Dale's story, tracking further developments in what had now become the ongoing investigation into the real-life drama of her disappearance.

There was still speculation that the whole thing was a publicity stunt, but it seemed obvious to Flynn that the concern voiced by the heads of studios, her agent, and fellow cast members, even if it was on nighttime entertainment shows, was no put-on.

Meanwhile, he and millions of others were treated to an ongoing opportunity to witness nearly every hot photo or clip of the star that had ever been made public.

It never ceased, the barrage of stills with her hungry eyes from her early roles, the glittering sight of her sheath-like designer gowns at various celebevents, her confident smile, cat-like eyes and purring voice putting more successful actresses on edge. A particular favorite was a paparazzo's shot of her unintentionally yawning as she was introduced to George Clooney at an "A-List" fund-raiser.

"Yo," called Barnaby, opening his door. Unsurprisingly, he went to the refrigerator and took out a quart of soy-milk.

"Hey," said Flynn. He couldn't help but read his roommate's t-shirt out loud: " 'Auto-tune Your Bullshit.' That a band?"

"No," said Barnaby, without further elaboration.

"Oh. So how's the filming going?"

"Pretty good." Barnaby surprised Flynn by coming to stand beside the sofa as he drank from the carton. No worries, thought Flynn, there was no way he'd be putting his lips on that, that was for sure. That was one plus about living with a vegan, there was no unintentional or intentional pillaging of each other's food. It was not likely that he'd come home after a night of drinking and scramble up some tofu that wasn't his. He decided not to bring up the bra in the bathroom from the other day, which was the only other thing he could think of to talk about.

"Yup. We should be finished by the end of next week. Fascists tried to shut us down but we were gone before they got there." Barnaby pitched the soymilk carton into one of the four recycling bins.

"Really? That sucks. How'd you know they were coming?"

"We get tips. There's a network."

"Cool."

Barnaby continued to stare at the screen.

"Like her?" said Flynn, referring to Dale.

"Did some great early stuff," said Barnaby, nodding. "Before the machine got her. Really primo. She should do something with DeNiro. Or, remake of 'Taxi Driver' but she plays Bickle."

"Sure," said Flynn. "Hope they find her."

"Yup," said Barnaby. "Yup," he added for extra emphasis, and went to the fridge to extract a huge bunch of celery and a bag of what looked like mung beans, both of which he placed on the counter. He plugged in the coffee maker.

"You gonna – " began Flynn.

"Keep it real," said Barnaby, heading back to his room.

"Great song! Even after, like, ten plays!" called Flynn.

Barnaby's door closed behind him.

Apparently he'd have a night of wailing guitars and, yet again, flushing toilets. When the fuck am I going to be able to get my own place, he thought, losing patience as after a slight, tantalizing break, the mammoth crescendos began once again. The irony of his being in real estate and yet having no real place to call home was not lost on him. Waking up to the smell of vegan shit might be one step up from a frat boy's hurl, but, still, it was glaringly obvious that his empty pockets were dragging him down into the gutter, and there were sure as hell no rainbows in sight.

He could smell the smell of sauce as he approached Nicole's building. The kind that simmered on the stove for hours. Like at his friends' houses. For a moment, he almost felt like he was seventeen again and going over to dinner at his best friend's. After football practice Mario would invite him over and there was nothing better in the world at that moment than sitting down in front of the steaming plate piled high; after, he'd have to fight falling asleep right there. When he'd finally drag himself back home, everything about the meal kept him warm inside, until he saw his father sitting by himself downstairs and knew by the silence that his mom was "not feeling well" again.

Her hair looked so silky and shiny he wanted to sink his fingers into it right there. Not to mention the dress. It had very, very thin straps, one of which had already slipped off one shoulder. And she was wearing heels, red ones.

"Hi," she said.

He was holding a bottle of wine and, yes, wearing a tie. She had been cooking for hours, and the smell of the garlic and the onions and spices and tomatoes simmering on the stove along with the wine she had stirred in quite liberally, as well as the sips which she had also consumed quite liberally, had gradually worn away her worries and fears, to be replaced by a broadening delight in all things sensuous, and right before Flynn had arrived, it had all reached a climax.

At first, as she began to get ready, it had popped into her head how much she wanted to hear some music, so she'd gone up to her studio and selected several vintage LP's bought out of pity on the street from an old jazz musician who said he was selling them to "feed his cats." Maybe, maybe not. It didn't matter, he needed the money. She'd made her selections based solely on the album covers; 1950's lone attractive women in black velvet evening gowns, staring soulfully off into the distance.

Then the "Broadway Cocktail Party," "for Dancing or Party Background." A handsome dark-haired man in a black jacket, white shirt and elegant narrow black bowtie pressed his face against the cheek of a blond woman in a voluminous white fur stole, who smiled triumphantly as if displaying her trophy after the big game hunt.

Flush with the wine and her burgeoning excitement over seeing Flynn, Nicole decided to take a huge risk and actually play this one. Without the copious wine in her system these records would have been slated for the instantaneous categorizing and calculating of worth, or more likely lack of it, that was the hallmark of any true native NYer. Whether bagel or band, judgment was automatically triggered like security systems in Greenwich, Connecticut. If Ned had been there, the "exaggerated emotionality of the era," would have been the first alarm, followed by the ironic acknowledgement of the "cool" cover, followed by the de rigueur laugh at the song titles, for example, "I Enjoy Being A Girl," (not) and "Hey There!" (the drunken slut or slimy man song!).

But instead, she'd found herself swaying her head and humming along to the tunes with their "schmaltzy" sound, and when it came time to choose her dress, she appropriately dragged out a floor length black velvet with a plunging back. Cocktail party style. But it had been too hot in her apartment for velvet. Reluctantly she'd taken out a thin and filmy dress from Italy, along with Italian red leather pumps from the 1960's. There were parts of the dress that were almost see-through so she'd chosen an ivory satin slip to go underneath. She had just been tackling the über-important selection of bra and panties when she had heard the doorbell.

Fuck! Out of the three pairs she'd laid on the bed she'd grabbed the most obvious choice, black, and then changed her mind and decided to go with one that hooked in the front, and stuck her feet into the shoes and fastened the straps and ran for the door and just before opening it to run downstairs and let him in she'd realized she'd forgotten to put on her dress. "OH. MY. GOD. NICOLE. REALLY???" she'd said out loud and run back and tried to slip into the fragile fabric without tearing it and then grabbed her glass of wine and taken a huge gulp. She'd clattered down the stairs and opened the front door and that's what'd he'd seen, her flushed and smiling face, laughing at her ridiculous almost-blunder.

Flynn smiled at her. "You seem a bit...breathless."

"Dress-less?" said Nicole. She started giggling. "Oh my God," "You wouldn't believe what I almost just did."

"What?" said Flynn.

"I almost – I almost ran out of the door without my dress on."

"Really?" said Flynn, raising an eyebrow. "Well, I'm flattered."

"It was a mistake!"

"Are you sure?"

He put his hands on her waist and bent down to kiss her.

Nicole had put tea lights in red glass holders, and, miracle of miracles, found two intact glasses.

"This wine looks amazing," she said, looking at the label.

"I've always liked it," said Flynn.

Ned would only have brought a couple beers for himself. Now *this* was what it was like to date a grown-up. She turned to him with a smile.

"Here's my favorite painting," said Flynn, walking over to a landscape of the Gowanus he'd looked at last time. There was a little red dot stuck on the wall next to it. "What's this little red sticker for?" he said.

"Oh, you're funny," said Nicole. "Don't worry. I'm saving it for someone. Not that people are beating down my doors. Pre-sale sale." She smiled archly. "It's a gift, silly."

"A gift? For me?"

"No, for Donald Trump. Of course it's for you. If you want it."

"If I want it?" Flynn came over and put his arms around her. "I don't deserve you. I really don't."

Flynn wouldn't let her drain the heavy pot into the sink.

"I'm used to it," he said, pouring the boiling water out and tipping the spaghetti into the waiting colander. "Doing things around the house like this."

"Oh," said Nicole. "What about your mom? Didn't she - "

"She wasn't really around," cut in Flynn. "Do you have a bowl or anything?"

Wow, fucked up parents are really a buzz kill, thought Nicole, as she reached for the Fiesta Ware. For once, she felt it incumbent upon *her* to lighten the mood.

"I hope you like the sauce," she said brightly, as they sat down. "I kind of invented it myself."

"It smells great," said Flynn. He dug into the food and was putting forkful after forkful of it into his mouth letting the taste and the warmth overwhelm him and then he remembered that he was here and not seventeen. He put down his fork.

"I'm sorry. I'm being rude."

"No, I'm glad you like it." She beamed at him.

"It just reminded me – I used to go to my friend's house after school and his mom would cook just like this and it was, it was so great...I was always starving after football practice."

Football? She was dating, and most likely about to sleep with, a guy who'd played football?? She had no experience in the "genre." Was there something special she was supposed to say after a guy brought up "football"?

"Wow, football player to art dealer. That's a new one. Well, I guess that's not true anymore. That probably makes sense," she rattled on, like a train aiming to become a wreck.

Flynn didn't answer, just kept on eating, and she realized she again must have fucked up, her endless ream of judgment coming out of her mouth like an uncontrollable stream of misdirected bodily waste. GOD. I AM AN ASSHOLE. IT IS LITERALLY IMPOSSIBLE FOR ME NOT TO BE AN ASSHOLE EVERY SINGLE SECOND.

Should she apologize? Should she ask him about sports?

In that moment, she realized that she was completely at sea in the realm of what most people would consider a "normal" conversation. One where you pretended a polite interest, or one in which the other person's speech didn't function purely to reflect and bounce off of one's own. The polite kind had no place in New York, there was no time, and who really cared about some other person's doings if they were not intimately related to one's own? The latter was the kind of exchange that was never light enough to be called "banter," containing as it always did what New Yorkers always confused with facts: their own opinions on everything under the sun. When two natives spoke amongst themselves, they either ripped each other's throats out or bonded in a surety of perfect, dark judgment that the rest of the world lacked the capability to understand.

Yes, she was out of her depth, if only in more shallow waters.

"I went to all these little places to get the ingredients," she offered. "There used to be a lot of small stores in this neighborhood,– you know, those little Italian places? The first time I went in one, I asked if they had grated cheese and they just looked at me like I had insulted them. They had to grate it for you. There was this great Polish place too. I could live on one of those Kielbasas for like a week."

Flynn nodded. "There used to be a lot more mom-and-pop places where I grew up too. Still are some, but not as many. Too many chains."

"Where did you say you were from?"

"Bay Ridge. My Dad still lives there. Same house where I grew up."

"I've – never been there. Where exactly is it?"

After the meal they went back up to the roof.

They kissed for a long time. He ran his hands over her body, but didn't make any attempt to take her clothes off. She touched the back of his neck, felt the clean cut of his hair, his biceps through his shirt. Holy God, she thought. There was no smelly rock t-shirt, no unwashed pants with worn-out backsides, no greasy hair, no flaccid unexercised arms. Why hadn't she always dated men like this?

She couldn't believe how good she felt. And it was not only that she felt good, it was the kind of good it was, the absence of certain components she had always associated with what she had mistakenly confused with pleasure. How was it possible, she wondered, to be so attracted to someone who wasn't mean to you in the sarcastic way that she was so used to, who was the farthest thing from the kind of male whose seduction involved subtly taking you down a few pegs; more often than not, a so-called liberal or radical whose actions revealed a misogyny that rivaled that of any self-proclaimed sexist. Whose snide put-downs were foreplay. What made guys like that worse was the necessary lie that they were cool with strong women. And what made it even worse, in fact the worst, was that she had gone along with it for years in her intimate relationships. She, a supposed feminist, who prided herself on her refusal to "take any shit" and her belief that she was always ready to kick ass against some egregious injustice involving the female sex. Right here, right now, the feeling with Flynn was so foreign, so oddly painless, that she almost felt like she was in a dream. They were just leaning back, against the roof, comfortable with each other, and she felt herself being lulled into sleep by the feeling of safety. *If there was no spike sticking out of his personality, no twisted hook, then where would she hang herself...*came the strange, half-awake thought.

She woke up with his arm around her and her head on his shoulder.

"What happened?"

"You fell asleep."

Nicole brushed the hair out of her eyes and sat up. "How long was I out for?"

"Just about a half hour."

"You sat here the whole time?"

"Of course. Are you still sleepy? Come on. Let's go downstairs. I think you need to go to bed."

He took her by the hand, even helping her down the ladder, lifting her down the last rungs.

In the apartment he started towards the sink and the pile of dishes and pots from the dinner.

"I'm going to wash this stuff up before I go."

"No – really – I'll do it," protested Nicole.

Flynn was already at the sink. "There's no water coming out," he said.

"Really?"

Flynn tried the faucet again.

"That's weird," said Nicole.

"Does this happen a lot?"

"Well, no, I mean, it's an old building...but..."

"Let me go try the bathroom...nope, sink doesn't work here either!"

"Tub doesn't work," said Nicole, investigating the status of her sanctuary. "Fuck. This place is falling apart. The other day the lights just went out all of a sudden. It's getting really creepy around here."

"I know," said Flynn, without thinking.

"You know? What do you mean?"

"I mean... I know how old houses can fall apart."

"Oh. You scared me for a second," she laughed. "I thought you were a stalker or something."

"Listen, Nicole, I need to tell you something," began Flynn, but she cut him off.

"You think this is bad. Last week I tried to open the window to the fire escape and it was totally stuck. I mean totally impossible to open. It was like it was nailed shut or something."

"Nailed shut? Are you serious? Did you look at it?"

"Well, there was no way because – "

"Of course. I'm so stupid. You couldn't get out there from in here." Flynn clenched his jaw. "I'm going to go outside and climb up there right now. Let me – I'll just go upstairs and grab your ladder." He strode towards the door.

"Wow. Thanks. I called my boyfriend but he – " Oops.

Flynn stopped in his tracks. "Your boyfriend? You have a boyfriend??" He stared at her.

"Well, the - the thing is, we're not really getting along and I, I'm not sure I, I mean I totally don't want to see him anymore," Nicole stumbled.

"I can't believe you. All this time you had a boyfriend?"

"I – I..." She tried to put her hand on Flynn's shoulder but he shrugged it off.

"Wow," he said. He gave a hollow laugh. "I thought you were different. I thought you were for real. All this talk about 'morality' and 'values', and how nobody cares about anybody else anymore. I guess that only applies to other people. At least when I pretend to be something I'm not, I'm not being a hypocrite."

"What? What are you talking about?"

"I'm not sure, anymore." Flynn began pacing around the room. "Well, you know what?" He threw up his hands. "This is great, actually. 'Cause I was feeling really bad, I was feeling really shitty. Here I was thinking I was the only one who – "

"Who what?"

"Who was a liar."

"What the fuck are you talking about??"

"Don't yell at me."

"I'm not yelling," Nicole yelled.

Flynn went and sat down on a corroded red velvet armchair with faded gold tassels and put his head in his hands. "Christ."

"I'm so sorry, I didn't know what to do, I just liked you too much- "

"You know what? Once I tell you about – well, what I, what I've done, it won't even matter. It'll be over anyway." He got up and went to the window and looked out at the buildings across the street.

"I'm not an art dealer, Nicole." He turned around to face her. "I'm a real estate agent."

The look of horror on Nicole's face was like that of a woman who has brought home a cute one-night stand only to discover that he is a serial killer.

"Oh my God," she shrieked. "I let you in here??"

"I – don't work for a gallery. I – I work for the developer who's taking over the block. It wasn't my fault – I was only supposed to go and talk to them downstairs and then –"

"What?? You work for the developer??? Somebody sent you over here?? Are you spying on us????"

"I was just supposed to talk to the owner – I was going to make her a final offer –"

" 'A final offer'?? What, an offer she can't refuse? Who the hell are you?? 'Real estate'? Really?? I know what that means. The ones that have the storefront 'offices' where the blinds are always down and haven't been cleaned since like 1957???"

Her vocal volume increased by several decibels. "I grew up in New York City, okay?? Manhattan. THE MECCA OF MIND POWER. THE BASTION OF BRAINS. I may not live there anymore, I may have gotten pushed out of my hometown by people like you, but I'm no idiot.

I'm no Bridge and Tunnel bonehead. Holy God, the lights, the water, the window?! What, you were going to leave a fucking horse head on my bed next???? Get out!" she yelled at Flynn. "Get the fuck out!!! I DON'T KNOW WHERE YOU'RE FROM, BUT I'M PART SICILIAN, OKAY? YOU. CAN'T. FUCK. WITH. ME."

Flynn's protestations and attempts to explain further got him nowhere. He was running down the stairs, almost afraid she would start throwing plates at him.

Flynn stumbled down the street as if he were drunk. His head was a whirl of pain and confusion. Why was everything so complicated? He'd just wanted to go over there, to see her, to be with her, he couldn't deny to himself how much he liked her, and then her revelation about her boyfriend had completely knocked the wind out of him. For some reason it was like Constance all over again. It was that sense that women were after all completely foreign, that under all their maneuverings and attempts to get attention and excite one's interest they really had no idea at all what it was they really wanted.

But it was ridiculous for him even to have these thoughts. Look what he'd done. Compared to his preposterous deception, her transgression paled. People had overlapping commitments and love affairs all the time – that was just reality, that was just the way it was. It wasn't every day, though, that you told the girl you were maybe falling in love with that you were completely someone else than you actually turned out to be.

CHAPTER EIGHT

Flynn hadn't made it up to the futon of death. He'd collapsed on the couch in his clothes after coming home numerous-drinks-at-a-dive-Irish-bar later. A sound that was unfamiliar was pulling him out of his alcoholic slumber. He blearily opened his eyes and saw what made him sure he was dreaming: Barnaby, in jogging shorts and sneakers, running in place.

"What?" he mumbled.

"What's up, brother," said Barnaby, reaching down to touch his toes and then stretching back up with his hands over his head.

Ugh. Flynn could still taste the combination of many layers of beers and sleep in his mouth and it wasn't pleasant. He sat up. "You jog?"

"Nope. Protest." Barnaby turned so Flynn could see his T-shirt, which read, "The Corporate Yuppie Fuck Run" and then spun around to show his back: "Bringing more wealth to the top 1% every day."

"We run the wrong way in the park. Fucks them up completely." He put on a face of grit and determination, slowed down his steps, mimicked speeding back up again torturously, then pumped his fists in the air as he passed through an imaginary finish line with his back to it.

"Take everything for themselves, leave the rest of us to be slaves to the machine," said Barnaby, in between simulated gulps for air. He jogged out of the room backwards.

"Have a good run!" cried Flynn.

All the events of the night before were swirling around in his head. Fuck. FuckFuckFuck. He went to the kitchen and took out his non-organic orange juice and made himself some toast with stale supermarket bread.

He'd fucked shit up, royally, and now, the question was, exactly how to unfuck himself.

He took a deep breath as he screwed open the lid on some instant coffee. His brain was streaming the requested data as if it had just ingested one of Barnaby's blender creations. He'd quit his job. Move away. No. Stay here. Get something completely different. Maybe his

Barnaby turned so that Flynn could see his t-shirt, which
read: "The Corporate Yuppie Fuck Run".

Dad could get him something in construction? How about the Fire Department? Or maybe a cop. Something less stressful than real estate. And Nicole? He'd go back to her with a clear conscience. Before too long, she'd see him in a completely different light.

Flynn turned on the TV and flipped through the morning shows as he sipped the bitter coffee he'd made for himself. Through his hammering hangover, he watched the anchors tackle their task of delivering the news that mattered: a major star had just had her second set of triplets – or was it her fourth set of twins? Another had cursed out and flung a roll of toilet paper at a bathroom attendant who was now writing a book about it; someone else was denying she had major reconstructive surgery while another actress was going on all the talk shows to sell every excruciating detail about hers. A reporter stood "live" in a familiar looking neighborhood, and the anchor was throwing the news over to him.

"It's a sad day here in Park Slope, Candy," he said. "Police have recovered items believed to belong to Dale Shaw, star of 'Open Heart Surgery,' who disappeared last week while on location filming, 'The Slope Also Rises,' in which she plays a seductive childless single woman who sets her sights on a married father of two whose wife is pregnant with twins after recovering from a bout with breast cancer in which one breast, tragically, had to be removed.

"Shaw's personal effects were recovered from the Gowanus Canal, among them, a bag with a cell phone police are hoping will give them clues to the identity of whoever lured her to the remote area, and who looks more and more likely to be responsible for what police say is likely, tragically, her demise."

A burly Irishman standing next to him now spoke, "We're looking at the phone to be our 'black box,' if you will," said the man, identified in a caption as Detective Murphy of the newly created CCS (Celebrity Crime Squad). "As of now we're still working on recovering its data. The toxic sludge in that body of water could kill Godzilla if he so much as gargled with it. But we're confident that we'll be able to restore any information that could lead us to the killer."

"Sad, tragic, and fascinating. Thank you Detective. Back to you, Candy."

Poor Dale! How awful! And to think that just days ago he had met her, talked to her, even talked of making a date with her... and left her that flirty and mysterious teasing message she probably never got, the one he had hoped would tempt her into an intimate, one-on-one meeting where no one else was around...

HOL-EEE SHIT.

He hoped to God they didn't fix that phone.

Nicole had been so pissed off and angry and down-hearted and then scared after Flynn had left that she'd gone upstairs and put on a Joy Division record, and used the "romantic" 50's LP's as Frisbees. She'd undoubtedly had both too much wine and too much drama, two things that were frequently in combination in her life. Call it her Italian heritage at work.

She shouldn't have trusted Flynn, you should never trust anyone, especially someone in a suit. How could she have thought he was sexy??? She was losing her values, the ones she was now feeling she had tripped over, the ones she was all screwed up about because of what he had said. But she would examine that later, the accusation of hypocrisy in her personal matters, something that beyond the occasional luxury croissant, she had never contemplated. Hadn't she always been pure, hadn't she always sided with the underdog and taken the sufferings of others on as part of her personal responsibility?

But of course she had been fucked over. Contrary to what she'd said, no, yelled to Flynn, she *was* an idiot. To believe that any true man could ever love her, and by the way, another voice in her head reminded her, he wasn't a true man at all, as if she knew what that meant anyway. Here she was thinking that Ned was a loser, at least he wasn't a criminal, unless you were counting his minor pilfering of certain streams of thought from archaic rock crits of the early 1970's such as Lester Bangs that were completely unknown anyway to the young readers of today. Whatever. Anyway, yes, anyway Flynn was a horrible, complete loser in every way, he flaunted his sexiness, unlike the flaccid rock-crit-boys and alt-rockers, he dressed himself up, in his shirts with their biceps, in his suit pants with their real, leather, manly belts, just to torture her and other unsuspecting women. Worst of all were his subdued ties and everything they conjured up – early James Bond, the men of the 1950's with their hard, knowing noir faces, who faced evil down coolly without breaking a sweat, got in their cars, slammed the doors without making a sound and sped off when told to go after the bad guy without even asking for the address. Men got brainwashed early with tons of tasty tart treats wrapped with sex tailored just for them to hypnotize them and sell them things – they had bikinis, spike heels, reams of bare bodies, lengthy hair and seductive glances, they were babes in the woods well trained to follow the trail of booty crumbs to the house of product, but girls rarely were given anything sartorial to salivate over and now the vision of a hot appropriately dressed "adult" male would forever leave a bad taste in her mouth. Real estate??? Of all the slimy, nauseating betrayals. He'd come here for the developer, seduced her, ATE HER SAUCE. And to find out what??? What could they possibly not know already? That the people in the building didn't want to leave, that they were displacing yet another group of what you might be forced today to call "challenged" New Yorkers, oh, it had nothing to with alternate Olympic Games, it was anybody that wasn't a soul-sucking spider that lived only to siphon the life out of catchable living beings, wrapping them up in their corporate webs and storing them for future feeding fests throughout the winters of low company profits.

In the wee hours of the morning she had curled up somewhere on the floor surrounded by her art, and drifted off into a half-sleep, her thoughts forming into mini-movies trying to turn into full-on dreams, partial pictures and accompanying words competing for space while her brain scrolled through stored thoughts and memories for night recycling and sorting. It was all like an unstoppable flood, visual bits and pieces of the struggle, when she'd first started to feel cornered like she was cornered right now, when she'd reached a point of what felt like final desperation, and should she do something like try to get some painting gigs for a corporation like make a huge painting for a huge office building lobby …her mind created that saleable picture that beckoned her, she saw it bright with lots of red and yellow and black like McDonald's, and she would be trapped against her will, the evil marketer whispering that there was a way out of the cage that was descending, and now she saw herself the secret agent in a TV show stuck between two mechanized walls closing in, but there were no cutaways to shots of impending deliverance and the walls didn't magically seem farther apart each time the camera cut back to her as she'd hold it from crushing her with outstretched arms and legs …but could there be a way to make the punishment of the painting fit the crime of the waiting masses whose crime it is to accept the product produced by the evil marketer who has sucked their brains out, studied them, and then genetically engineered Trojan horses of manufactured culture from the cells of slaughtered laboratory mice known as artists... but many had had the idea of trying to fool the marketplace into supporting them by feeding the lion the red meat of their butchered dreams while trying to be a vegetarian on the side...

CHAPTER NINE

In a congruity with his son that had perhaps never been reached before, Harry did not make it into work on Monday. Joy of joys, Mrs. Haliburton had finally called, making her apologies and asking if perhaps they could go back for another lunch to that restaurant they'd gone to before.

"It's just so nice to be at a place in New York where the entrees aren't the size of our finger food," she said, as they settled into the comfortable banquette seating at the Blue Ribbon.

"I completely agree," said Harry, and he meant it. Since her phone call to him, he'd been in a mood that could almost be described as "bouncy." Everything appeared more fun to him, less fraught with the ever-present potential of projects going horribly wrong. He hadn't felt this kind of drive since before the debacle of his failed movie aspirations.

Helen Haliburton stirred her long glass of ice tea with an even longer spoon. The sheen of condensation on the outside was cool, wet and trickling down the side, the perfect antidote to the heat of 5th Avenue. And the perfect addition to the antidote was the best grade of bourbon the house could offer, mixed in very liberally. The bartender had prepared the mixture according to her sweetly given "suggestions." Floating on top were succulent slices of orange.

"I don't mind admitting that I like my drinks strong, Mr. Harmony," she was saying. She removed the spoon and laid it down lightly, raised the glass to her lips and took a tall, satisfying, but still ladylike swallow.

"In fact, back in the South, when Mr. Reagan came into office, and everybody short of the local militia was called a 'liberal' for some reason or other, I would always have to remind folks that the only thing I am liberal about is the amount of good whiskey I like in my drinks."

She smiled across the table at Harry, who, wrestling with his conscience, had gone with a white wine spritzer, one of his rapidly dwindling token concessions to weight loss.

Harry grunted. The use of primate-like sounds for communication was habitual, but it was dawning on him that a woman like Mrs. Haliburton might not find it impressive.

"Ha-arry," said Mrs. Haliburton, drawing out the name as if to increase its importance. "Thank you again for bringing me to this lovely spot. That looks promising," she said, as a waiter passed by carrying a platter supporting a formidable cut of meat.

Their waiter, a startlingly handsome young man who introduced himself as Ted arrived to recite the specials of the day, each one flaunting a more mind-boggling juxtaposition of tastes than the last. Harry watched jealously as Helen complimented Ted on his memory and delivery.

"Are you an actor, Ted?" she inquired.

"No, ma'am," said Ted. "I was an editor at the City Section of the Times, but things are rough out there right now."

"Oh, you poor dear," said Helen. "Now, we will have just the plain old-fashioned filet mignon we saw passing us by earlier. How's that sit with you, Harry?"

Harry thought fleetingly of his increasingly unlikely choice of a Caesar Salad, which he thought, if only because of its name, could possibly pass as manly. "Perfect," he grunted. "So, what is your daughter looking for, exactly?" he asked, trying not to stare at the basket of rolls and pats of ice cold butter that had been set down on the expensive linen in front of him.

"Harry," said Helen, transferring a roll to her side plate and breaking a piece off without dropping a crumb, "it's not so much what she is looking for but what *I* am. If she had her way she'd stay right where she is, I'm sure. She's quite enjoying not having the lifestyle to which she had never become accustomed. You see, I only married Carl when she was twelve." She deftly smoothed the butter onto the roll.

"I fell in love with him despite, not because, of his background. He had a good heart, I could see that. He let me go all out when it came to charity and philanthropy. But his money was a weight on him. He was never sure just what to do with it all. It was all inherited, you see. That's never good for a man. Doesn't let him find out who he is." She chewed in perfect close-mouthed bites, her lipstick unsmudged.

"My father had a sausage factory on Bergen Street," said Harry.

"Really?" said Helen.

"Yeah. Then he bought a few buildings, got some tenants. But it was a small operation. I'm the one who built it up." He took a sip of the spritzer and frowned at its unsatisfying nature.

152

"Well, isn't that *interesting*," said Helen. "And I imagine it was your hard work that put your company on the map."

"Exactly," said Harry. "As a matter of fact, I'm working on a project right now. This one's *really* going to raise our profile, if the goddamn tree-huggers don't get in the way of it. Excuse my language."

"Well, and isn't it always those who are the most self-righteous who turn out to be the hypocrites," said Helen. "When my car breaks down by the side of the road, give me a so-called 'redneck' any day. He'll be the first one to pull over and help you, mark my words."

Harry nodded. He was liking this woman more and more.

"I'm going to have a nice condo for your daughter," he said, suddenly losing control and seizing a roll. "Gorgeous high rise right down the street from here. Glass, steel, 24 hour doorman. Upscale grocery, dry cleaners. She won't even have to leave the building. You should have seen this neighborhood when I was a kid," he continued, warming to his subject and forgetting not to speak with his mouth was full, "Gangs, drugs. Don't get me wrong, there were a lot of good families around here. But you had to move out to move up. Who wants that?" He reached for another roll.

The filet mignon was set in front of them.

"Oh, look," Helen said to Harry before the waiter could leave, "you've just about finished your drink. May I recommend the one I'm having? It's my own recipe. I'll be offended if you don't!" Her laugh tinkled lightly. The smile-and-casting-of-her-eyes towards Ted was all that was needed to send him scurrying off bar-bound, to return mere moments later with an extra glass and a full icy pitcher.

"Compliments of the house, Ma'am," said Ted. "Jorge said to tell you if he had his way he'd make this a special summer drink named after you."

Jorge could be seen behind the bar grinning and waving at Helen.

"Now isn't that adorable. Tell him as long as he keeps my recipe up North he can go ahead and do what he likes. Y'all need better ways to relax up here. It's Haliburton," she said to Ted. "Haliburton, with one 'L.' "

"Here's to our friendship, Harry," said Helen, raising her glass. "I was just about despairing that I would find a man I could talk to." She watched as Harry tasted the drink.

"Excellent," said Harry, controlling a near-gag response to the outrageous amount of whiskey in the so-called "tea." It bothered him that she had referred to what he thought of as a date as their "friendship."

"I'm going to tell you something about myself, Harry." She laid her soft manicured hand on top of Harry's larger and somewhat flabbier paw.

"You may not have noticed, but I have an effect on men. But I would never in a million years misuse that privilege. Yes, I was the one who persuaded Carl to drop the second "L" in our name. He knew I was right, of course. We had to distance ourselves from what that name had become. It wasn't a *family* name anymore. It was owned by a company that wouldn't know right from wrong if it gushed up from an oil well and painted their clothes black. Yes, dropping that second "L" was like ripping out one of his organs, Carl told me, just before he died. But it set us back on the beginning of reclaiming who we were. Values, Harry, good old-fashioned values. That's all we have that sets us apart from the things we hate."

She began to cut her way into the steak, whose brown and red juices oozed out and wafted their aroma into the air.

Harry nodded in agreement, but in truth, his brain had been put on hold temporarily, courtesy of the newly-dubbed Haliburton Ice Tea, the delicious prospect of enjoying a forbidden meal, and the complexities of Mrs. Haliburton's conversation. How had they made the near-impossible leap in subject from condos to values, he wondered, taking another swig of the high-proof thirst-quencher. Never mind, he was enjoying himself in ways that were far beyond taking meetings, barking down politicians, and weighing whether to fork over an extra hundred dollars for a post-massage hand job.

"I couldn't agree more, Mrs. H," he said, lapsing into a Brooklyn colloquialism.

For the first time that day, Helen Haliburton did not look pleased, but she recovered quickly.

"Why don't you call me Helen," she said.

Score one for me, thought Harry. Beyond his bold and rare plan to pick up the check, he was now ready to offer further proof of his affections.

"Helen, here's to your daughter's condo," he said, raising his glass. What better way was there to show a woman how you felt but to offer to hook her up with prime real estate?

Since he had become star struck by his new dream of entrepreneurship, Buzz's focus had shifted from the task of keeping hidden while blowing poisoned darts at his father's exposed neck, to the excitement of planning this next venture. His last nefarious activity had been to rifle through the list of Harry's contacts and pass them on to the representatives of whoever was paying him, but meanwhile, he had become so enamored of his updated idea of pet ownership that he had mentally checked out on that job as if it was his latest trick. He'd never be an effective wrong-doer; he just didn't have the attention span.

One could say it was a step up for him if only his invention hadn't been so repugnant. Everyone knew that there was a type of urbanite who used dogs as accessories for various benefits: chick or dick magnets and trendy status symbols being the top two. But Buzz felt the time was right for such a practice to come out of the closet, as it were. Why be ashamed? Why keep the motivation hidden? It was only natural to admit, nay, to capitalize on the modern need for constant change as well as to acknowledge that as one's fortunes rose or fell, or for that matter, one's weight, heels, or the height of one's hair, one ought to be able to vary one's accoutrements to best advantage. Polydogamy, you might call it, since you would be "owning" many different dogs. The reality was this would only be taking a certain mindset of self-concern to the next level, and the way he would begin, would be to open a chain of pet stores with full-length mirrors, in which you could rent your dogs. Why had no one ever done this before? He could hardly believe it, but it seemed to be the case. Since people sized you up and passed judgment almost instantaneously in this town, the right dog to match your looks, demeanor, and apartment should really be taken more seriously. For just one example, what if the black poodle you just purchased for three thousand dollars actually accentuated the curly hair you had been trying to smooth down for your entire life? Or made your encroaching gray or thinning areas more obvious by contrast to its own young, full, richly colored coat? Rule #1: never buy a dog prettier than you. The last thing you wanted was for the eye to travel up from the dog to you and rapidly, disappointedly, scroll back down. That could explain the explosion of pugs: there was no way they'd make you look ugly. With this new angle, there'd be no commitment, ever. Perfect. He could cater exclusively to gay males if he wanted. There'd be no risk of ever being tied down, in the wrong way, of course, "married" to your pet. Rick Santorum, who had insisted that the next demand after legalizing gay marriage would be a move to tie the knot with one's pet, would now have nothing on the gays. He'd have to get investors, flesh out the idea, of course, but that shouldn't be hard to do. The timing was perfect.

"Xanax!" he yelled, and the newly-named animal came dashing out. Since their dual mirror-gazing, a rapprochement of sorts had been reached. Buzz felt he had found a partner in his vanity, plus the prospect of a non-monogamous relationship with his dog had already made him feel less trapped, happier, more relaxed. Hence the name.

He hooked Xanax onto his black leather studded collar and leash and issued forth onto the streets of Chelsea, letting the animal poke its nose into all manner of tree bottoms, gutters, and bases of street lamps. The fire hydrant had fallen out of fashion years ago, for some completely unknown reason.

As Xanax sniffed, Buzz checked the continued availability of his beloved target apartment online, as well as his stocks, and the current range of offers for his apartment in the East '30's that he'd put on the market in his drive to have ready cash for the dowry of his domicile. He contemplated the rest of his day. To the gym for a workout, where he could most likely get a blowjob, if not two, then buy some clothes in those lame designer stores in what once had been the original Meatpacking district – what a great name that had been, when there were people who could truly appreciate its meaning… then what? For an odd moment he experienced a feeling of emptiness. He really didn't have any friends. He yawned. In lieu of anything else and because looking like you were looking for something to do was for losers, he went through three of his usually neglected email accounts, where he saw in one an invitation to join the latest online connection and communication "community", where you could post your whereabouts constantly, as if anyone gave a shit. Out of utter and complete boredom, he actually bothered to click on the link, and it turned out that you were rewarded with points each time you posted your whereabouts if they were on a certain list, and the points added up for the types of coupons banks gave you to get stuff that you were supposed to want – various trips, with a million and a half restrictions in mitochondria-sized print, digital electronics that would be obsolete tomorrow or already were, gift cards to huge chain stores that were limited in different annoying ways; the usual assortment of things that weren't worth the trouble. But it was free.

"Cool," said Buzz out loud, and joined ISquat, typed in his current location, which was by a participating bank, and then thought for a moment before adding the required one or two sentence personal elaboration on one's moment-by-moment activity. He didn't want to reveal too much about himself, he was too cool for that, plus of course, rich, and if he really blogged about what he was doing he might get stalked or someone could try and rob him. Not that he was stupid enough to post that he was at the ATM.

His dog snuffled with his snout in a particularly pungent place and let out a happy bark.

"Found a friend?" said Buzz sarcastically, and typed in, "On a corner in Chelsea. Xanax is checking his pee-mail."

Even his dog was upscale and technologically savvy.

CHAPTER TEN

How do you say fuck you in smoke rings?

By Wednesday, Nicole had spent three nights completing her newest creation, and she contemplated this question as she hammered the last nail into the huge easel-like structure she'd erected on her roof. There'd have to be some way for her to communicate with the world at large once she'd settled in with her sandbags, and by sandbags she meant all the goods and supplies she'd been dragging up the stairs. Her water had never come back on, and the electricity had been spotty, at best, lighting up and then flickering off in a downright eerie way. So she'd dug herself in: the gallons of bottled water, the candles, food in cans, and, most importantly, the Chianti. Yes, she was settling in for the long haul. She would not run like a scared little rabbit. She would not be driven out of her home yet again, but if, in spite of her best efforts, it did come to that, she would go down with her artwork raised up high behind her and a glass of wine lifted as a final salute to the once great and now soulless city. She'd have one last look at the sunset setting behind the skyline, the view of the Island that had once been hers, a source of inspiration, now to be sold to the highest bidder, the glass condo walls framing the panorama that now meant nothing more than dollar signs. Say goodbye to her hometown that had betrayed her and so many of its artists who couldn't march in time to the new tune. Wondering if it really was cool in Portland, Oregon. Or was that Portland, Maine?

The strains of David Bowie's "Diamond Dogs" issued from her studio, the outdated turntable and speakers giving the music a punch and a depth that made it seem three dimensional in comparison to the digital age. That fucker was loud. Just turn it up to four and it could blast through the whole house. Loud enough for a disco party on the roof, if only disco hadn't sucked. "Any day, now…any day now…" chanted Bowie, and Nicole chanted along with him, savoring the lyrics with their apocalyptic predictions and depictions of stratified urban hunting grounds, the warnings of a world that was already here, the phrase, "Young girls, they call them the Diamond Dogs," being particularly gratifying.

"Come out of the garden, baby, you'll catch your death in the fog…" and it was in fact cloudy and damp, but Nicole was impervious to the unpleasant weather, she was doing what she loved best, and that was painting and hammering and making things, and now that she'd made this monstrous frame she would have the extreme pleasure and luxury of deciding which paintings to hang on it for the world to see, which ones with the biggest "fuck you" content, or would she choose the joy of making new ones, throwing herself into her work with the excitement that can only come from knowing that it will be ON DISPLAY, MOTHERFUCKERS.

"THE FUCK YOU TRYPTYCH," that would be its name. She would tack on the last word just to be pretentious so maybe the art dealers would come, who would then run off with their tails between their legs when they discovered what she now envisioned as a Goya-like mural full of mutation and fantasy, ultimately communicating the sense that life was so out of control that no one, not even the bastards who had taken over this town, could really do much at all that truly mattered, once nature had taken her course. They would all be mutated and flushed, too, one day. But that was neither here nor there.

"You want a show???" she yelled from the roof. There was one more question to answer, and that was where she would go to the bathroom when she ran out of the bottled water she was using for flushing. Urine as medium had already been explored, so perhaps she would grace Starbucks with her presence for the first time.

There had been no "right time" yet for Flynn to give his notice. Harry hadn't been in the office at all on Monday, and when he did come in on Tuesday, he disappeared like the white rabbit and shut his door.

But today was Wednesday, and Flynn felt it was now or never. He might end up working in Starbucks - he'd heard they had medical coverage - but at least he'd done the right thing.

Flynn knocked. "Sir?"

There was no answer.

Flynn opened the door cautiously and was hit with a blast of cigar smoke.

Harry had his feet up on his desk, and was staring off into the distance in a meditative trance.

"Mr. Harmony?"

"Hmph?"

"Can I talk to you for a minute?"

"Sure. Have a seat."

Flynn sat down obediently.

"Well," he began.

"Kid?" Harry broke in. If the trajectory of his gaze, which was focused feet above Flynn's head, was any indication, he hadn't returned from his contemplation of the great beyond.

"Sir?"

"You know what love is?"

"Uh –"

"Love is never having to say you're busy."

"Oh. Okay."

"So, what can I do for you?"

"Um, well, sir, I've certainly enjoyed my time here…but I, well…"

"You're getting out," Harry cut in.

"Yes, sir."

Harry sat up in his chair and opened a box on his desk. "Have a seat."

Flynn was already sitting.

Harry took out a cigar and held it out to Flynn, who felt he had no choice but to put it in his mouth. Was this the bone Harry had been waiting to hand him?

"Kid," said Harry, flicking on a lighter. "I don't blame you. I myself may be turning a new corner in the near future."

He paused for the effect of his announcement, and Flynn felt obliged to display interest.

"Sir?"

"You ever seen 'Gone with the Wind?'"

Flynn broke into a fit of coughing. "I think I saw part of it on TV once."

"What would you think about a version from the slaves' point of view? You know, modern, PC, don't want to offend anybody. Think about it." Harry described a large arc in the air with his hands. " Clooney, Pitt, maybe Halle Berry. We make it set in today. Brooklyn. She plays the nanny. The woman she works for is trying to pop it out right there. So she says, 'Excuse me, lady, but I haven't been trained as an obstetrician.'"

"Sure," replied Flynn. "Look, uh, sir, about the building - "

"The building, the building. Listen, I'm not gonna do a thing about it right now. Remember what you told me about the underground railroad? I have been spending time with a very exceptional woman. Turns out, she has an interest in historic houses. I told her about it, she's very interested."

"Well, actually," began Flynn.

"Hold on, I'm getting a call. It's her! Helen, how are you? Good luck, kid," he called out to Flynn, who realized the meeting was now over. He left the room, smoking cigar in hand.

"Niiiiiiiiccccccceee," called out Seth.

"Celebrating something?" asked Kev. "You pregnant?"

"Haaaaaahhhaaaaaaaaaahhhhhh," they laughed.

"No, but your wife is," replied Flynn.

"Nnnnnniiiiiccccceeeee," said Seth. "In with the big man. You get a promotion?"

"No," Flynn answered, crushing his cigar out in Seth's Hooter's mug.

It was almost dusk. Had he done the wrong thing? He'd cut himself adrift with no lifeboat. He'd have to move back in with his father unless something fell right into his lap, and soon. Above all, he couldn't face John Bonham's drums for one more night.

He found himself stopping in front of Cregan's, an old Irish bar that had been on Fifth Avenue for decades. Through the open door the smell of stale beer-soaked air and the ineradicable odor of cigarettes built up for years before the ban wafted out; it was dark and nearly empty. He hesitated for a moment, but was drawn in by the feeling that by entering he was leaving the world that had pushed him into turmoil and inhabiting a space where none of that mattered.

A long, piercing look from a dark-haired man sitting all the way at the bar's end would have unnerved him had he not felt quite so numb. All he wanted to do was sit and stare and drink. To be one of those men you could always find at bars like these, sitting there for hours every day starting at noon, thinking about God knows what, or maybe not thinking at all. Whether it is nobler to try to understand all the unbelievable crap of life, or to let it flow off your back like oil off a spill-coated duck.

Fuck it. He ordered a Bud.

Little did he know that by his choice of beer he had distinguished himself from the disliked yuppie and hipster males who were now making increasingly frequent forays into bars like these, seeking the dwindling authenticity of the City and yet demanding small-batch brews only recently introduced and considered laughable by a large segment of the born-and-bred Brooklynites.

"That's a good beer," the man at the end of the bar said, "but Guinness is better. Tommy, give him a Guinness."

The bartender flicked a rhetorical glance at Flynn as he set a pint glass under the tap and began the long, slow draw.

"Thanks!" said Flynn.

The man was silent.

Flynn smiled uncertainly. There was something about the man's quiet gaze in his direction that put him on edge.

It was silent as a church while the stout was taken through its many stages, the man at the end of the bar watching each angle of the glass, the interim settling of the foam, the final filling.

When it was ready, and Flynn raised the glass, he was reminded for some reason of Communion. Only that was less serious since it had been really meaningless to him and the other children, full only of jokes about drinking the wine and about being hungry for the wafer. He had a feeling that witticisms about Guinness, unless you were a part of some inner circle here, were not welcomed in this place. He took what he hoped looked like a large confident swallow but came out more like an unplanned gulp.

The man at the end of the bar had raised a finger as his own Guinness had dwindled to a couple of inches. He stared at the new pint as it sat in front of him for what seemed like ages. He then drank at least a third of its contents in one easy go.

"Jimmy Cregan," he said, turning to Flynn.

"Flynn Sharpe," said Flynn.

The man nodded. "Flynn. What do you do?"

"I – used to be a financial analyst. Wall Street. Got laid off, though."

"Banker, huh?"

"Well, more like moving money around for bankers."

"Times are tough, huh?"

Flynn took another draw from his glass. "Yes. Yes they are."

Cregan kept crooking his finger and the beers kept coming and then at some point shots appeared too. Flynn had lost count but what he did know was that at some point he became one of those men he had thought about earlier sitting there for what seemed like forever except that he wasn't silent like they were. He was the guy at the bar who was spilling it all: about Nicole, about Constance, about how he had gotten mixed up in all the real estate chaos and deception, about how he wasn't getting his due, about his dwindling financial resources and how different that was than just months ago when the money was flowing like four-hundred dollar wine through the two-foot-long neck of a Stone Street decanter. In spite of how drunk he was getting, he managed to keep his embarrassing impersonation of an art dealer along with the stupid trendy accessories out of the story. That was the kind of wimpy modern man maneuver that, far from impressing him, would be anathema to a guy like Cregan. Slick moves like that might go down well with a newer breed just blocks away; you could shift into a whole other strata of society with completely different values, if you could call them that, by moving an avenue or two over. But Flynn's instinct screamed bloody murder at him to just shut it when it came to the shaky subterfuge he had engaged in. It didn't seem smart right now, it seemed weak.

He kept talking, and as he talked about it all it seemed like its ridiculousness was just amplified, how he had waltzed unknowing and naïve into a cesspool that he should have been smart enough to avoid. How had he sacrificed his own good judgment just in trying to get a leg up? And now he'd lost her. Who? Cregan's steady stare was like a magnet that drew the words out of him like poison sucked out of a snake bite. Oh, the girl.

He answered every question the bar's namesake asked him. Once or twice he tried to turn the conversation around to the other man, but for reasons he couldn't quite recall he abandoned that pretty quickly. It was when his eyes became heavy lidded and difficult to keep open that

Cregan startled him by moving to the bar stool next to him, sitting there motionless just as he had when waiting for the right moment to lift his Guinness, and then putting his arm around Flynn suddenly in a comradely fashion that nevertheless scared the shit out of him.

"You ever make soup?" he asked.

"Shoup?" mumbled Flynn, who was now completely three sheets to the wind.

"Yeah, soup. My grandmother used to make it when I was a kid. She'd put in the chicken parts and the vegetables and the water and I'd watch her stir it and it'd start cooking, and it'd smell great. But then you'd start to see these little bits of grease and fat everywhere. This dirty grayish-yellow foam, floating up to the top. You ever see that?"

"Can't shay I have."

"Yeah. So she'd take a wooden spoon and she'd start to skim it off. Sometimes she'd even let me do it, you had to be careful or else they'd get away from you. And it'd start to look fine and perfect, like you'd got it all out, but then you'd give it another stir and more scum would come up all over again. It was always hard to believe there was still more." He leaned closer. "But then, we'd get the milk and back then it was in bottles not the crapshit paper it is now, glass bottles the milkman left for you outside your door in the milk crate. And if I was a really good boy, I'd get to have a taste of the buttery part that was right under the cap. See, that's what can get you crazy." He put his face next to Flynn's. "There's two things rise to the top. The scum *and* the cream."

Buzz was loving ISquat like hell. Imagine this heaven! People actually wanted bulletins of where you were and what the fuck you were doing every single second. Of course! This was perfect for him. It was about time! And Xanax's burgeoning internet popularity, had grown by leaps and bounds in a matter of hours. It was keeping Buzz occupied, but not enough to stall his ever-present hunger for The Private Penthouse Home featuring 2523 Sq.Ft. of Breathtaking North and East Birds Eye Views of the Empire State Building, several East River Bridges, Brooklyn, and Beyond with Sparkling, Brand New Features a PRIVATE 5,000 Sq Ft ROOF PARK, Swimming Pool/Hot Tub, Squash Court, ½ Basketball Court, Gigantic 25' Ceilinged Health Club, Bowling Alley, Locker Rooms with Saunas, Yoga Room, (who the fuck needed that, but at least it didn't have a fucking children's playroom) Business Center, and Screening Room and All with Full Service 24-Hour Doorman and Concierge who would probably procure you whatever the fuck you wanted at any time of the day or night for the right amount and also could possibly be a trick who knew? AND the frieze of the Discus Thrower who was the ultimate fuckable fantasy and would get everyone he brought home ready to go just by looking at it with WALL STREET JUST AROUND THE CORNER!!!!!!!!!!!!!! in the FINANCIAL DISTRICT!!!!! that WON'T LAST!!!!!!!! but it had ha-ha and he was currently hovering over it, a vulture over the virtual prairie of new stakes, waiting to swoop in at the right moment following the death of the asking price.

"Quiet!" he yelled at Xanax, who had watched his owner long enough to have acquired one of Buzz's most persistent habits, and was now out on the terrace of his Chelsea condo eyeing the street below and commenting, in dog speak, on the parade of like animals below.

Right now he was letting out a marathon snarly bark, so long and unstoppable that Buzz was forced to cease his online monitoring of his desired dwelling and the other units in the building and nearby neighborhoods and the progress of their market status.

"SHUT UP!" he said, coming to stand next to his dog and following Xanax's rabid stare to the object of his attention.

"He is so not worth it," he said, in what was evolving to be an almost fatherly way, or rather, a combination of cruise buddy and parent. "Trust me, he's probably a mutt. You're not a mutt queen, are you?"

He navigated to ISquat and logged in. "Xanax is cruising a mutt off the terrace. Ugh!" He then snapped a quick pic of Xanax's snout through the terrace bars pointing down to the street below, even managing to include the tail end (literally) of the object of his dog's affection (and/or rage, it was really quite hard to tell) and sent it off. Then, realizing that he himself frequently had a taste for several different "combinations" or "blends," as far as ethnicities in men went, he, in perhaps his first ever instance of familial empathy, added, "Like father like son! What can I tell him, keep it on the DL!"

Yes, Xanax had gone viral, as the notice of his about-the-town doings in tony-trendy Chelsea had spread like kennel cough. Xanax's S & M stylings were particularly popular, and Buzz had even received a text from a huge designer's rep looking to use him in a trademark skeletal-rich-people-dabbling-on-the-edge-of-decadence photo shoot. Other users were posting pictures of their dogs in hope of a future match (Xanax was un-neutered), adding captions like, "Helmut my daschund is a total bottom who needs a good daddy!" and "Kiki's ready for the leash!" etc.

This pleased Buzz to no end, and he even thought of launching a doggie fashion line – most important would be the upscale leather and stud line of leashes, collars, etc., then maybe little hoods and why shouldn't their booties that they'd need in the cold be black leather also? There was even a potential trick who'd just emailed him who claimed to be a designer who had already designed a special outfit just for Xanax, and who was offering to come over now with the gift. Yeah, I'll take your gifts, both of them, thought Buzz, smirking, and sent him his address. Add that to the fact that all kinds of shit sold online these days. Why not doggie t-shirts with catchy phrases like: "What would Xanax do?" or "You've got pee-mail!"

Like a proud papa he threw the rising doggy star a treat and watched while his surrogate progeny inhaled it. "You're on your way to stardom, bitch!" he called out, then, for the first time in his life, felt he had used the b-word inappropriately.

There were some things in life that you couldn't understand unless you were Tanked with a capital "T." Blind. Pissed. Legless. Gone. Done. Hammered. And one of those things, pondered Flynn, out on the street and leaning against a storefront, was that unless you were drunk, you couldn't understand the truth of that.

Every time he'd had a surfeit of whiskey and Guinness, he'd ask himself why he didn't do this more often. Drink, that is. It opened his eyes. Helped him see the big picture. Understand the true essence of things. This wasn't how he'd think about it the next morning, granted. But there were a precious few moments, or was it hours, during which he could be certain he'd found the meaning of life, or love, or just why it was that one's job sucked, and that an even deeper understanding could be found by following up this drink with another.

And the essence, was, he realized, that he wanted Nicole. Now. Like, Right Now. It was all a stupid misunderstanding. So what if he didn't have a job anymore, and was about to end up homeless or living with his dad. The thing was, they should be *together*. Having hot sex.

Making passionate love. Whatever. Whatever the fuck it was okay to say now. She couldn't still be mad. In fact, he had a brilliant idea. He'd text her! Why wait another moment? How about, "Let's have hot sex right now!" She'd totally get it. Because he really did care about her, he might even love her, but you didn't say that over the phone.

He felt for his cell, but instead of finding it, his hand surprisingly fell on a bump in his jacket pocket. It was Nicole's turquoise, sequined slipper, still where he had put it the day he found it.

Wow. He'd forgot all about it. Was this kismet or what? It was a sign! The luck 'o' the Irish!! He'd go to her right now, her Prince Charming, and it would fit perfectly on her foot. No doubt.

He lurched away from the wall, smiling, waving the slipper aloft, and as often happens when a burden is lifted, he also smiled at the first person he saw, a Middle Eastern man who was the proprietor of a store and newsstand, and who was standing outside next to the stacks of morning papers, smoking a cigarette. The shop owner smiled back and his ash fell onto the front page of the Daily News. Flynn's eyes followed its trajectory downwards, to see the day's headline, stark against the morning light:

ACTRESS KILLER'S CHILLING MESSAGE: HE'S
"THE ONE WITH NO STROLLER"

Holy God! Shaking, he pulled one of the papers from the pile: STORY ON PAGES 3-6. There it was, an entire four-page spread, with plenty of salacious shots, and a much, much smaller amount of print:

Cont. from p. 1 **NO STROLLER**

Late yesterday afternoon, police working round the clock to solve the mystery of Dale Shaw's heartrending disappearance got a break in the case: a message left on a cell-phone belonging to the TV star found along with other personal items last week floating in the Gowanus Canal, near where she was last seen alive. "We had to call

ACTRESS KILLER'S CHILLING MESSAGE

HE'S:
THE ONE WITH NO STROLLER

in the HazMat guys to help us clean it up," explained Police Detective Robert Farley.

The phone was placed in an isolated chamber and treated with chemical compounds in order to counteract the effects of the near-nuclear cocktail of waste that is the notorious body of water.

"Whatever's in that Canal ate away most of the device in just a matter of days," he explained, but efforts by experts finally restored the digital recordings. "God help us if we actually find the body."

Police would not release the entire text of the message, but did say that no name was left by the caller, who referred to himself only, alarmingly, as "The One With No Stroller." According to Detective Farley, the message was an attempt to lure Dale to "out-of-the-way places."

"This is a very sick individual we're dealing with right now" said the Detective, adding that most disturbing of all was the caller's brazen declaration of his twisted plan to get the star alone, somewhere where he could "breathe down [her] neck" without fear of anyone getting in the way.

How and why Ms. Shaw found herself in contact with such a person or whether she had previously known her attacker is still in question.

"Until the suspect is identified and apprehended we will continue to withhold any information that could jeopardize the investigation," concluded Detective Farley. "But we're getting closer to an arrest every minute."

Flynn dropped the paper and his jaw at the same time.

He saw his future before him, being hauled away with his hands cuffed behind his back, loudly protesting that he had an alibi: he had been a) at a lesbian bar, and b) masquerading as another person entirely.

Those not-too-sane sounding details of his whereabouts, coupled with the undeniable recording of his voice extending what out of context sounded like an invitation from your friendly neighborhood psycho, could be the perfect guilty storm for a media more hungry for sensation than fact. He would be convicted and hung in popular opinion quicker than a witch on a jet ski. Meanwhile, the killer would still be out there, haunting the Brooklyn waterfront, endangering everyone who came within his reach.

He had only one way to save himself and the other potential innocent victims from this embryonic disaster of epic proportions: he had to find Dale's killer, and he had to do it fast, before the police found him.

In her sleep, Nicole became conscious of a growing nausea…she felt sick to her stomach like she was going to throw up…it felt real like she had to wake herself and get to the bathroom… she was going to go out like the only cool hippie ever, Hendrix, but choking on the vomit of her thoughts …and from Hendrix the dream naturally became that she was in San Francisco, and she was in a house that started shaking and bits of plaster began to fall from the ceiling and a Buddha on a shelf became covered with plaster dust and then toppled over and broke because people on the West Coast have things like Buddhas in their houses, and being from Manhattan she had no idea what to do in an earthquake… and see this is what happens when you leave New York and go to California…

And then she woke up and in fact the building *was* shaking. A monstrous crunch and rumble, a huge inhuman groan and the shifting of some great mechanical brute. It could only mean one thing. The bastards were bulldozing.

"Oh, no, they di-unt," said Nicole, getting up faster than she had in years, sans coffee, fiercely mean, the fear and uncertainty fleeing her body as the prospect of a fresh battle surged through her vintage-clad personage. She pulled herself up the steel ladder in seconds and whacked open the trap door. It was already light outside.

"Shitheads!" she screamed, even before she could take a look at what was actually going on, and when she did, she saw that the bulldozer was still several buildings away, but indeed, the jaws of the Tyrannosaurus Rex of the construction industry were open, hungry, and about to take a massive bite out of the remains of Mr. Valle's shoe store.

"FUCKERS!!!!" She stamped her foot. Was her painting ready?? It was the first time she'd looked at it in daylight – and now it stretched before her, a gigantic mural, the initial panel of the triptych the remains of her pigeon paintings with the Manhattan skylines blurred from the dripping, and the birds and the cats and the famous buildings all melted into each other, misshapen and stuck together as if after a great conflagration, the second panel, a pyre made of her Gowanus paintings, with their brilliant, deep, earthy colors, the charcoalblackbrown of the water towers, the skies of light grey, palest blue, whitest yellow, the murky green depths of the waterways, old bridges and the tops of church spires.

The third panel was empty except for a few thick strokes of black paint that she'd started to lay across it before she had almost passed out with exhaustion. Well, too late to change that now. Looked like it was SHOWTIME.

Harry took Mrs. Haliburton's hand as he opened the door to the white convertible he had rented for the day. It had been her idea to get a very early start, when the morning air was still cool and fresh. He would take her on a tour of the mansions and the houses in the historic districts of Brooklyn, then, where else, Peter Luger's.

"Will you look at that!" said Helen, sipping on the Starbuck's Harry had splurged on for both of them. "Indians! So charming!"
They were driving by the Montauk Club on Eighth Avenue, a stunning Venetian Gothic palazzo, built in the nineteenth century and bearing the name of a local tribe who were depicted in friezes.

"What a gem," said Harry, hoping to gain her approval.

"Thank God for the preservationists," said Helen. "You know, I'm thinking of forming a committee myself."

"What a wonderful idea!" said Harry, nearly careening into the oncoming traffic. "And speaking of such important things, I could show you a few of my condos, especially," he added hastily, "the site with the underground railroad."

"Perfect!" said Helen.

"Yeah. You know, I was thinkin', the building goes up around it, we could make that part of the mall! Tourist attraction, sell souvenirs, maybe a ride, like a train, it goes into a special tunnel? We'd be raking it in!"

"All for charity, of course," said Helen.

"Of course!" said Harry quickly.

As they sped up Fourth Avenue, Harry went so far as to take one hand off the wheel and casually lay his arm on the back of the seat. This was how it was done. The girl. The convertible. The sun shining. Two stars in their own movie, filming on location in Rome.

And then, as they neared his development site, he couldn't believe what he was seeing. THIS WAS NOT IN THE SCRIPT.

"Oh, Harry, you didn't!" exclaimed Helen, as they both took in the sight of the ravenous bulldozer tearing chunks out of the side of a tottering concrete wall.

Harry was speechless.

"No, I didn't," he gasped, when he could finally speak.

He scrambled for the door handle.

"What the fuck???!!" he yelled over the noise, throwing open the car door and running down the block maniacally like a frantic bird trying to protect its brood. "I didn't authorize this! Stop it! Kibosh! Stop the fucking machine!" When that didn't have any effect, he stepped directly in the path of the bulldozer.

"I'M THE ONE WHO GETS TO CONDEMN THIS SHIT!" he screamed. When the man behind the controls remained oblivious, he tried to remain standing where he was, but the mammoth wheels were turning dangerously close.

Scampering out of its way, Harry shook his fist angrily.

"WE SHALL NOT BE MOVED!!" he vowed.

Not surprisingly, fear in the Slope that day grew rapidly in response to the media's revelations, with the result that already by late morning adult men who were seen to be unmarried and without children and WITHOUT A STROLLER were viewed with rising suspicion, much as women in the same position routinely were, and their usually rock solid stock as eligible bachelors regardless of looks or income took a nosedive.

"That is so sick, that he would say that," was the childbearing chorus from Starbuck's to Kidville.

"It's like he's purposefully targeting us, like everybody else is, for no reason at all."

"I've always thought that guys like that were so weird," said one of the twenty suckling mothers taking up three-quarters of the seating and tables in the Tea Lounge. "You see them, walking around by themselves, no wedding ring, it's creepy. Especially if they're in their late twenties or older, and they still aren't married."

And indeed, it was creepy, particularly for the white men who found themselves the object of frightened and/or angry stares by other white well-off suburban and Upper East Side implants, being treated almost if they were black men similarly dressed.

"We're just human beings like anybody else!" one sans-ring and tattered backpack and jeans type in his late thirties couldn't help but protest outside Starbucks, surrounded as he was by stares. "A week ago you would have thought I was cool!"

Flynn, meanwhile, was unaware of this spreading new form of bigotry. After a few moments of desperate thinking, he had made his way West, towards the Gowanus. The trick would be to stay out of sight for as long as it took him to clear his name. A cop car had cruised past him as he'd stood on Fourth Avenue waiting for the light to change, and he'd had to stop himself from bolting right there. He had to be careful not to draw attention to himself. It was a good thing he was wearing his suit; he could be just another Wall Street bound yuppie on his way to the "R" train. He was sweating by the time the interminable light changed, and he was able to cross the street. Keep calm, keep calm, he told himself, as he came to the bridge over the Gowanus, where his cell phone suddenly rang and he just as suddenly panicked and tossed it into the water.

Harry was in full-on rage mode to anyone who would listen. His little black book of contacts seemed to have mysteriously disappeared, which at any other time would have been enough to send him into an apoplectic fury, but today, its possible theft was no match for his outrage regarding the apparent takeover of his property. "WHERE'S THE OUTRAGE?" was a phrase that he had seen often in the media, but he hadn't paid much attention, as he had generally been the detached and distant recipient of said anger, and not the self-righteous injured party. But now, he knew where it was. It was right here, in the face of this egregious injustice.

And so, after the ghastly experience of trying to get in touch with anyone important via "normal" channels, and having had, for the first time, to try the much-advertised 311, (that was like the fucking Poseidon Adventure, like floating through the flooded engine rooms of the incompetent city government like the albino flipperless rock seal that was Shelley Winters, ineffective and doomed) he had charged in person straight to where he thought his complaint would be received with consternation, matching incredulity, and immediate steps to action. When real estate tycoons talk, the City walks, but he almost had a heart attack right there outside City Hall, when, after composing himself enough to give his name – which angered him even more, shouldn't they somehow, already be aware of what was going on? – he was told that no one was able to see him, and advised to call 311.

"AAAAAAAAAAAHHHHHHHHHHHHHHHHHHHHH!" screamed Harry, whereupon he was dragged through a metal detector once again for good measure, given a pat down and escorted out of the area by two looming security men with curly cords behind their ears.

"WHAT IS THIS, RUSSIA????? WHAT IS THIS, THE FUCKING KREMLIN?????" People stared at him as if he were crazy, a ranting raving lunatic instead of the wrongfully denied citizen that he was. "I KNOW MY RIGHTS!!!!!!!" he shouted, and with this declaration, surprised even himself. Did he, in fact?? Knowing your rights only came in handy when you were about to lose them, and if you were about to lose them you probably hadn't been paying much attention anyway. Would he have to find out about them now???? Would he have to call up one of his many lawyers to learn what they were? Which one of them would know? Maybe not any, because they were versed in real estate, finance, personal injury, and other like important causes only. Civil rights hadn't been on the menu.

His day had continued as a bizarre marathon of phone calls, but each time he managed to make contact with an actual human being, he was dropped down another rung: "talk to so-and-so," "call this department," "I'll transfer you." The options menus closed in on him like an escape-proof high security jail; he was left to rot in the solitary confines of recorded "Just a moment, please,"s, followed by endless lengths of time - humiliated, forgotten, a prisoner of the Guantanamo Bay of the hold button.

At one point he found himself literally beginning to snarl like a rabid wolf, his jaws wide and the saliva gathering by his gums. Helen, who had taken it upon herself to keep an eye on him during this "unpleasant" time, took the receiver from his hand.

"Take a breather, Harry," she said, beginning to rub his back.

She must have unknowingly touched a chakra, because he dropped his hands to his lap and sank back into his chair. He smacked his lips for an instant as if a fat farm-yard pig had just outdistanced him.

"I've called everyone, Helen," he said, dully. "Two, three, four times. No one wants to talk to me. All of a sudden I'm Oscar Mayer olive loaf in this town. Two of my lawyers – I got their answering machines, and they don't have them."

"You're havin' a bad day, Harry, that's all. Everyone does sometimes. Have a pastry."

Harry sighed and reached for an éclair. "I guess you're right, Helen. Hey – could be some goddamn government bureaucrat. City employees, they're a joke, and everything's computers now – some moron presses a button, now they're bulldozing the wrong block. See what happens when you give someone a pension?" He took a mournful bite of the chocolate confection. The phone rang.

"Yeah, this is him," Harry said, with his mouth full. "Who's this?............ What do you mean that's none of my business? Are you trying to squeeze me? WHAT? WHO HAS THE RIGHT TO DO THAT??? ....Oh, yeah? I'll hit you from here to Hoboken! I'll whack you from Weehawken to Wichita.....EMINENT DOMAIN??? YOU CAN'T DO THAT! IT'S AGAINST THE LAW! OH, RIGHT............. SOMEONE WANTS TO TALK TO ME HUH!? NO, *I* WANT TO TALK TO *HIM*---- WHOEVER THE HELL HE... is... ....Oh.....................................Okay..... Yessir.. .... I understand...Nooooooooooo ooo problem...no problem-o..........nope, no questions.... You have a nice day too, sir.... And God Bless America."

Harry hung up and looked dazedly at Helen. He was silent for several seconds.

"I'm not a big fish anymore, Helen," he burst out, finally, hanging his head. "The whales are comin' in... and I'm plankton."

"You got leaned on, didn't you?"

"But I'm not supposed to – tell – I've got express orders, I mean, I was 'advised'…" Harry's voice sank to a whisper, and he scanned the room as if expecting to see a government agent standing behind the curtains.

"Homeland Security. Or House Energy Committee. I couldn't tell which. He said it very quickly. They want access to the waterway." Here he snuffled, unable to go on, his dreams of "The Venice Mall" shattered.

"Is it terrorist threats?" asked Helen, biting into a pastry perfectly.

"No. They said 'fracking.' First I thought he was cursing at me. Gas drilling. It's gonna be the biggest thing ever, he said. Said once it starts for real it's gonna make the California gold rush look like a Sunday trip to Home Depot. He had a voice like, like John Wayne after being dry for three days," continued Harry. "He said if I keep my mouth shut I'd get a piece of it, and if I didn't, they find me under 'a ridge of shale.'"

"Sounds like it could have been Rex. Rex Dichter, he was in Carl's circle. Or was it Dex Richter? Yes, yes, I think that was it. HUGE oil man, and of course then it goes without saying one of the top men in HS. The two just go together like a Hostess Cupcake and the cream inside of it… or maybe Juniper P. Johnson … Hard to know. Their voices all sound like that." She took a measured sip through the cinnamon. "Maybe even Dickie. Now I thought he'd retired. But you know, these men never really do, Harry. Not as long as there is money to be made. You'd find them one foot out of the grave if they could, once a new prospect comes in sight. They'd get the word even in heaven. Or elsewhere…Anyway, I wouldn't worry about it. I wouldn't believe all of it, either. You never know just what they really want, and you'll go crazy trying to figure it out."

"I'll take the shares," said Harry quickly, as if he'd suddenly made a measured decision.

"I wouldn't sit on the edge of your seat for it," said Helen.

When, after nightfall, Flynn emerged from the derelict warehouse that he'd selected for his cover, he need not have worried about being spotted. It was pitch-black, darker than he had ever seen the city before. It was a no man's land here, without street lamps or homes to light the way.

He'd found a spot by a dead end, a place he was sure he'd remain undiscovered as he contemplated his next move. He had to concentrate. Focus. *Creep like a cat.* Cautiously feeling his way over the terrain that was, despite outposts of wealth such as condos and artisanal feeding halls, still dotted with treacherous cobblestones and crumbled curbs, he made his way closer to the banks of the Canal.

Ah. Yes. Here it was. He could tell by the fetid odor, the damp and cold that penetrated the air around the still and stagnant waters. And yet they were deep, and murky, and the recipient of God knows what horrible evidence of God knows what horrible crimes. It was now time to begin his work: of watching, waiting, using the keenness of his senses and his raw instincts to flush out the perpetrator. Poor, poor Dale. What a way to go, here, in this place where your cries and screams would never be heard, just another woman victim like all the ones without which TV crime shows would not exist, to exit this world as merely part of a forensic expert's paycheck. He'd avenge her death, bring the killer to justice. He stood tall, hands on his hips, in the style of a determined celluloid detective. He only wished he at least had a protein bar. A calorie-boosting snack would be just the thing to sharpen his wits.

Headlights pulled into view out of nowhere. He heard the crunch of wheels on gravel and then the sound of slamming car doors. He slunk to the ground as two policemen, their radios beeping and crackling with official communiqués, shone their flashlights up and down mere yards away.

God! No! Please! he prayed, and some deity must have been watching, because after a few moments, they turned back, got into the car, and drove away.

But now he heard helicopters overhead.

He was shaking. The shaking, hiding, murderer, that's how they'd find him. He began to run, his footsteps echoing on the cobblestones. A safe haven – a place to hide – and there it was, what looked like a dark opening leading into an even darker space, but it was shelter, and take it he must. Once inside, he leaned against a wall, gasping for breath. Safe, he breathed to himself, safe at last.

But suddenly a spotlight exploded over his head, and he knew they'd got him and he was in their sights, but seconds later he was wishing they had, because here, right in front of him, was a monstrous vision: the rearing platform of a front loader, coming straight for him, and at its controls, the killer himself, head down and face hidden by a hard-hat, Freddy in construction drag. Flynn stumbled backwards in terror, where he fell directly onto a moving conveyor belt and heard the steel blades of an industrial saw begin to turn.

"No! No!" he cried, in his final moments, looking up to see his executioner bearing down upon him without mercy, and then, taking off the hard hat, and shaking out a long cascade of shiny, luxurious auburn hair - and it was Dale.

"CUT!!!!!" came Barnaby's annoyed voice, and he stepped out of the shadows. "Yo, man, WHAT'S UP? You ruined the shot."

Half a bottle of shared chilled Icelandic vodka later, Flynn still couldn't believe what he was hearing.

"So, you were never in any danger at all?" he said, leaning back against a digital editing machine in the film crew's van that was parked inside what he had found out was the illegally accessed Dyke's Lumber yard.

Dale sucked the juice out of a lemon slice and threw back another shot.

"Only of dying of boredom. Seriously, I just couldn't go through with another bullshit demeaning part. So when Barn and his crew rolled up in their van, I was like – ROAD TRIP! Out of *that* hell. These guys – they totally appreciate my work. Well, the early stuff I did like five years ago. Okay, ten."

Barnaby didn't drink, so he just nodded. "Yup. She was totally being wasted in those sexist roles."

"But – but what about the clothes in the Canal, your bag, the phone??"

"Dumped it," said Dale. "Done, you know?"

"And you were hiding this whole time? Where?"

Dale giggled.

"Right under your nose, man," said Barnaby. "With me. In my room. Behind the wall of Zep."

Flynn's eyes widened, and he remembered the bras hanging in the bathroom.

As if reading his mind, Dale said, "Yup. Those were mine!"

"I didn't look at the size, I swear!" protested Flynn.

"Too bad. You could have sold my real measurements to the tabloids. Oh," she added, picking up a newspaper, and turning to Barnaby, "did you see this? I'm thirty-nine. Again!" She tossed it to the side. "They can kiss my forty-six year-old ass!"

"Right on. And the best thing about it is," said Barnaby, with more enthusiasm than Flynn had known he was capable of, "she lived in the East Village when it was still cool. When it was the Lower East Side. Check this out." He held up an old, tattered t-shirt that read, "Die Yuppie Scum."

"Vintage early '80's!" he announced.

Dale ruffled his hair affectionately. "Wait 'til I show you the upside-down martini glass on that piece of the lamppost I got in the Tompkins Square Park riots!"

"You're amazing," said Barnaby.

"He's jaded about the right things and not jaded about the wrong things. He gets me," Dale said to Flynn as he climbed out of the van. "By the way, it's not sexual. Surprise! Some people just want to be my pal."

Flynn left behind the mutual admiration society that was Barnaby and Dale, and walked unsteadily into the breaking dawn.

Nicole was sleeping when she heard the sharp, insistent sound of a dog, barking over and over again. She opened her eyes, and it was then that she smelt the burning and saw the twisted curls of smoke creeping under her door. The building was on fire. She ran to the window. But of course, it wouldn't open.

When Flynn reached Fifth Avenue, even the vodka he had consumed couldn't transform what he was seeing into a castle inhabited by a waiting princess. Instead, what he saw was an old, collapsing building with smoke rising ominously from its roof.

MOTHEROFFUCK. Flynn reached for his phone, then remembered that it was now, unlike Dale, currently residing at the bottom of the Gowanus Canal.

"Help! Help! Fire!" he called out to the deserted street, and two vehicles, a Hummer and a Lexus, passed by, but neither slowed its pace.

"What the hell??" he yelled in desperation after their disappearing license plates.

At that moment a rugged, beat-up truck rounded the corner, and Flynn recognized the retired firefighter at the wheel.

"Mr. O'Connor!!!! It's me, Flynn Sharpe! Help!!!!"

It wasn't long before the news got out and the TV crews arrived, reporters prowling back and forth, helicopters appearing in the sky for overhead shots. This was indeed Breaking News, a fire being always deemed by producers to be the perfect way for city inhabitants to start their day.

Nicole had quickly been pulled to safety, Pat rescued from the basement. Now it was just the firefighters fighting the fire.

Flynn and Nicole stood, watching the blaze.

"It was a million dollar view, and now it's gone," said Nicole.

"No, it isn't," said Flynn, "I see it in your eyes."

Reporters circled the pair. "It was just you in there?" one pressed Nicole.

"Me and Pat. Her girlfriend owns the building. She was living in the basement. The developer was trying to get them to sell. She's in a wheelchair!"

"A disabled lesbian?" said a female anchor, frantically gesturing to her camera man.

"Black, disabled, lesbian in suspicious blaze," another wrote hastily on his pad, despite the fact that he hadn't seen Pat, who was white and Irish.

"I heard a dog barking. He woke me up."

"A hero dog!" salivated a writer for the Post. "Where the fuck is it?"

"Xanax!!!!" Buzz was running down the street, buttoning the fly of his leather jeans. He had spent the night entertaining a series of tricks in his boarded-up basement boudoir, and Xanax, who had become too dominant to be leashed, had trotted off hours ago in search of his own adventures. "Xanax, where are you??? You bastard!! I didn't mean it about that poodle!"

As the crowd stood looking on, Xanax, clad in a pair of leather doggy-chaps, came running out of the flames. He was carrying something in his mouth.

"Oh, God, no," said a cameraman, turning away from his lens, referring to the confluence of the chaps and Xanax's unneutered state. "That's disgusting!"

"Stand back!" ordered a cop. "This may be evidence." Xanax dropped his present at the man's feet and began to bark furiously.

"Oh, hell no!" said the officer, picking it up.

It was a CD of NWA's "Fuck Tha Police."

"That's funny," said Nicole, "That isn't mine."

Three firefighters came rushing out of the building just as it caved in completely. "There's a body in there," said the tallest, most strapping man of the bunch. "We were too late."

There was a range of people in various positions of power whose asses were saved by the discovery of the corpse's identity, not the least of which was Nicole's now officially ex-boyfriend, alt rock critic and campaigner for the Little Weevils, Ned.

What an incredible ending for the Weevils' story, better than Cobain's.

For it was Fidel, the smallest of the Little Weevils, who had been found, as Ned wrote, "burned, not beyond recognition, but by the lack of it. He died with his fuck finger raised" (although some said it was just the way his hand remained after a bottle had been twisted out of it post mortem). "He left us surrounded by his inspirations: Thich Nhat Hanh's *Vietnam: Lotus in a Sea of Fire*, George Harrison's "All Things Must Pass" (original double album with full lyric book), and Public Enemy's "Welcome to the Terrordome." In a final act of defiance, he dispatched the NWA masterpiece "Fuck Tha Police (signed 'To Fidel, —my wigga wit attitude - Dre) to the masses, as a symbol of ultimate resistance, in the living jaws of a one-headed Cerberus."

Altogether, an ambitious rock critic's wet dream, and Ned was poised and ready to frame the band's tale in the invaluable setting of vanished integrity, and "the courage of a monk immolating himself in protest," as he spun it, but no one would ever know if Fidel had simply fallen asleep, soaked in booze, smoking hash brought back from

Amsterdam in Nicole's cabinet where he had been squatting, and where Nicole stored her incredibly flammable painting supplies. At any rate, law enforcement declined to investigate further. It was to be Ned's career-making book, and with the advance from it plus the points he had on the Weevils' records, poised to bullet onto the charts, as records by dead rock stars are wont to do, he and Brenda could move in together and buy that place in the East Village where Iggy had his condo.

He already knew how he'd end the book:

"Don't curse the darkness, light a candle: that was Fidel's message. But don't do it in a cupboard. Let your light shine."

EPILOGUE

Xanax became an even huger internet star after dramatic footage from the fire was posted on YouTube; Buzz made an offer on his dream condo that was accepted, but was told the building didn't allow dogs, prompting him to declare that he'd call them back.

Dale and Barnaby pre-sold non-existent apartments in Brooklyn using Dale's star power. Ignorant potential investors with billions made from unsavory sources were treated to a tour of the "hot new" neighborhoods the duo had christened themselves: BHod, an acronym for "by the Brooklyn House of Detention," which was of course, never explained, and BoHiCa, which could have been Boerum Hill/Carroll Gardens, but was well known to members of the military as Bend Over Here It Comes Again. They donated all proceeds anonymously to the ACLU, before disappearing into the vegan/animal rights underground.

Pat and Sally used the money from the insurance payout from the fire to open a bed and breakfast/group home for homeless LGBT youth. They live in Queens and Provincetown.

Harry's dream of remaking "Gone with the Wind" was never realized. He and Helen started a business restoring historic houses instead.

Kev and Seth's band, Maximum Bird Slaughter, almost got to play at Spring Break.

Jimmy Cregan is still sitting in his bar if you want to talk to him.

Flynn and Nicole moved to the Bronx, where Nicole could still afford a painting studio. She made him promise that if they ever got married, they'd never name their kids Porter or Parker or Walker or Taylor, and then went into a rant on how, "It's funny how they are all names of service economy jobs. Park my car, lift my bags, walk my dog, fix my shirt! I wonder why their parents never noticed that?? Or maybe they *did.*" Flynn opened up his own practice as a financial planner in a storefront to serve the local community, and gave Sean O'Connor and all of his buddies from Farrell's free financial advice for the rest of their lives.

Made in the USA
Charleston, SC
19 January 2013